CW00410748

A CHILD OF AIR

A CHILD OF AIR

Alan Clews

Copyright © 1995 Alan Clews

The right of Alan Clews to be identified as the Author of
the Work has been asserted by him in accordance with the
Copyright, Designs and Patents Act 1988

First published in 1995
by HEADLINE BOOK PUBLISHING

A HEADLINE REVIEW hardback

10 9 8 7 6 5 4 3 2 1

All rights reserved. No part of this publication may be
reproduced, stored in a retrieval system, or transmitted,
in any form or by any means without the prior written
permission of the publisher, nor be otherwise circulated
in any form of binding or cover other than that in which
it is published and without a similar condition being
imposed on the subsequent purchaser.

All characters in this publication are fictitious
and any resemblance to real persons, living or dead,
is purely coincidental

British Library Cataloguing in Publication Data

Clewes, Alan
Child of Air
I. Title
823 [F]

ISBN 0-7472-1279-1

Typeset by
Letterpart Limited, Reigate, Surrey

Printed and bound in Great Britain by
Mackays of Chatham PLC, Chatham, Kent

HEADLINE BOOK PUBLISHING
A division of Hodder Headline PLC
338 Euston Road
London NW1 3BH

A CHILD OF AIR

One

When I was a child, I used to spend the summer holidays at my aunt's in Millarston, a village about twenty miles to the south-west of Glasgow. The countryside around there is mostly hills and moorland. If you climb those hills on a good day, you can see the sheen of the Firth, and the Atlantic stretching away towards America, broken only by the dark shapes of Arran, the Mull of Kintyre and the islands beyond. From the village itself, though, all you can see are the hills rising round you like a crowd of angry adults round a child.

My uncle was a farm labourer and he and my aunt had a cottage in the village. My own family lived in a two-roomed tenement flat in Paisley. There were five of us altogether in those two cramped rooms – my parents, myself and two younger sisters. So it was simply a matter of

3

practical convenience to pack me off to my aunt's whenever the opportunity arose.

I, for my part, raised no objections. Life was much easier and more comfortable at my aunt's than it was back home. I had a room to myself and there wasn't the same sense of money being eternally a problem as there was in that damp, dark tenement with its outside toilet down half a flight of cold stone steps and used by everyone else on our landing. Also, and most importantly, my aunt, who was much older than my mother and had no children of her own, spoiled and indulged me in a way that my own parents either wouldn't or couldn't. (At the time, with childish selfishness, I'd have said 'wouldn't': in retrospect, of course, I realize that 'couldn't' was the bare, brutal truth, no more palatable to them than to myself.) The simple fact is – and it is relevant – my aunt and I had a very close relationship. I was as fond of her as I have been of anyone in my life. Just as I was as happy then as I have ever been in my life.

Those summers – running through, I suppose, from about 1955 to the early sixties – were long, empty and strangely pleasurable. The only remotely unusual feature of life in Millarston was the woman with the bell.

You could hear the bell every afternoon at five. It was part of the life of the village, so much so that you hardly ever thought about it – well, at the time, I certainly never thought twice about it. All I knew was that the woman who rang the bell lived in the half-ruined big house that stood a mile or so outside the village. She came out once a day, always at the same time – five o'clock in the afternoon. She walked round the walled garden at the back of the house, ringing the bell every few moments as she went. There was never anyone else in the garden with her. The house itself was virtually falling down at one side, as if part of it had been destroyed by fire. When you saw it up close, you were surprised that anyone could live there. She'd stay outside for perhaps half an hour and all the time she was out there she'd go on ringing the bell, over and over, to the same slow rhythm.

Like most of the other children in the village, I had been told to stay away from the big house. I was especially warned by my aunt, and the warning was reissued each time I arrived at the beginning of June. There was a particular intensity in her voice whenever she mentioned the woman or the big house. I don't think I'm imagining that or simply layering it on because of what I know now. In any case, the warnings were, of course, totally ignored. If anything, they only served to deepen my curiosity. There were also the stories which I heard from the village children and which, at the time, I believed totally – as only children can believe things. Among the ones which I can remember were that the woman with the bell could kill people by simply looking at them (this was why she carried the bell – to warn people away); that she had magic powers and could fly, or at least jump great distances, so that if once she got onto you or chased you, you could never hope to escape; and that she roamed the hills at night looking for children to kill and eat. (People swore they had heard the bell at all sorts of odd times of the night – I'm still convinced I heard it myself several times when I woke in that small bedroom at the head of the stairs in my aunt's cottage but I could simply have been imagining it.)

I went to see her once. There was myself and a brother and sister called Henryson. The girl and I were about seven, the boy a year or two younger.

We approached the big house from the back, taking advantage of a bank of old pines to give ourselves cover. Some of the trees straggled close to the high wall that ran round the garden. As I remember, we used one of these to get up onto the wall. We slithered along the top to a bush or a branch which both concealed us and gave a good view of the house and garden. The house looked almost derelict. The windows on the upper floors were either bricked up or boarded up.

It seemed like hours before we heard the first ring of the bell and saw a door open at the back of the house. A woman in a long red coat or cloak came out of the door and down a short flight of steps onto a gravel path. In one hand, she held a bell. It was the kind of bell a teacher might use: brass, about six or eight inches long, with a straight wooden handle. She would ring the bell every few moments, lifting it slightly and then letting it drop back down again, almost as if it were too heavy for her. She didn't look around or take any interest in the flowers or bushes that she passed. She walked to the part of the garden furthest from the house, where there was a broken down old summer house. She sat there for a while and continued to ring the bell all the time. I can't remember anything about her face.

After about twenty-five minutes, she came back down the garden and into the house, closing the door behind her. Only then, finally, did the bell stop.

There had been many times during this when we had giggled or trembled with fear and come close to giving ourselves away. But now that it was over we felt a strange chill and suddenly, without a word being spoken, we dropped awkwardly from the wall and began to run, silently, without looking at each other, terrified that she was going to chase us. We stumbled and fell in the deep heather. But we were no sooner down than we were up again, no one wishing to be left behind the others. It wasn't until we were well away from the house, and back in sight of the village, that we collapsed breathless on the ground. We didn't say anything much at first. After a while, our nervous tension found some release in laughter. But it was strained and unconvincing and we all felt it would be a long time before we went to the big house again – if ever.

I have one other memory of the woman with the bell, which I have never forgotten and never will. It was one afternoon towards the end of a summer when I would have been eight or nine at the most, which would have made it 1957 or 1958. There were only another few days until I went back home. The weather had been poor for some time: cold, wet, lots of mist. The other children I normally played with were kept near to home so they could be sent out at the first break in the weather to bring in the hay. This particular day, it had stopped raining about midway through the afternoon. I jumped at the opportunity to get out, away from the house and be on my own. I took the rod though I knew I was unlikely to do much fishing. It was a prop, something to carry with me, a reason for going out on an afternoon that promised so little. Besides, you never knew, you might just settle down and find the fish were keen to take the bait that afternoon. My aunt wrapped me up in a scarf and a heavy leather jerkin that someone had sent over from Canada many years before. She told me to be back for tea and warned me to make it sooner if the mist or rain looked like settling in again. I went to see if the Henrysons, the brother and sister, could come with me. But they were, as I expected, out with their father, bringing in or drying off the hay.

A Child of Air

I went up onto the ridge that ran between two of the lower hills overlooking the village. You could see the big house from up there but I paid it no particular attention. If the things I'd seen there were strange, they were not (to my child's mind) any stranger than some of the other baffling glimpses I'd had of the grown-up world. I threw stones at some rabbits but didn't manage to hit one. I watched the burns for fish and even put the line out once or twice but with no luck. I passed an hour or so in this way. The mist would come down. I'd be lost inside it – lost in another world where everything looked different, where all landmarks had suddenly vanished. I liked that. It was a good and very welcome feeling. But then the mist would lift and I'd be back in the old familiar world. Finally, around five, the mist came down and stayed down.

I was not unduly worried. I knew the hills well. I also knew that all I had to do was follow the slope of the hill and that would lead me to the village or one of the farms or even the road. As soon as I came across any of these, I'd find my way easily back to my aunt's.

I could see about twenty feet all around me. No more than that. There was plenty of light in the air. You just couldn't see very far. I came down after a while onto ground that was more or less level. In doing this, I must have traversed the hill rather than coming straight down. It's impossible to have any bearings in that kind of mist and you cease to be able to judge distances or even time. So it was impossible to know just how far I'd gone or how long I'd been walking. I still wasn't frightened at this point: I had absolutely no reason to be so. But, somehow, instead of walking towards the village, I must have gone over towards the big house.

At least on the hillside, I had the impression of going in the right direction if I just kept moving downwards, even if in fact I was wandering way off course. But on the level moorland, I was far less sure of myself. I didn't recognize any of the ground or landmarks around me. And the more I went on, the more I began to feel a sense of alarm. I tripped and fell once or twice. I sank into mud way past my ankles and soaked my boots. Once, I did this with my right foot and the boot I was wearing came off, held fast by the mud.

It was while I was putting this boot back on that I heard the bell. It sounded very close. I was sure she was out there in the mist.

I started to run almost instantly. I hadn't even finished tying the lace of my boot. I'd hardly gone a few steps when the boot came off again and the bell sounded again. If anything, it seemed to be even closer.

I pulled on the boot and tied the lace as quickly as I could, looking round me all the time. I ran blindly ahead, though I'd no idea in which direction I was going. I could still hear the bell. Loud and piercingly clear. I turned in another direction and ran that way for a few moments. I tripped and went sprawling down a small gully, cutting myself and tearing my clothes. I landed in a burn at the bottom. And the bell sounded again. Still as close, if not more so.

I picked myself up and stumbled on through the burn, now in tears and with absolutely no idea of where I was or where I was going. I didn't recognize the burn at the time though I know now exactly where I was and had been there many times before to fish. I moved over to the far bank but the ground was steeper there and I wasn't being careful or rational so I couldn't find a way up. The bell sounded again. I was utterly convinced she was coming after me. She would be able to hear me splashing. She could probably see me too, even though I couldn't see her. I finally scrambled up out of the water, utterly terrified.

I heard the bell again. This time it seemed to be in front of me. How could she do that? How could she be in front of me now when she was behind me a moment ago. I started to cry. I didn't dare turn back to the burn. She would be able to trap me there. So I took off to one side, hardly able to see for the tears in my eyes. The bell sounded out again. There was no escape. I just stopped. Fell to the ground, weeping, waiting.

But she never did materialize. And, of course, she never was out there in the mist chasing after me. That was only happening in my own overheated imagination. She would have been walking round her garden as usual. I had ended up much closer to the house than I thought. And the sound had carried uncannily clearly in the mist. It all had a perfectly rational explanation. But that was no consolation to me at the time. And, I have to say, it was quite a few years before I realized that this was the true explanation of that terrifying afternoon.

When I was fourteen, I stopped spending my summers in Millarston. We'd moved to a bigger house in one of the housing schemes on the outskirts of Paisley so there was less practical need for it. Also, I suppose I'd more of a life of my own.

I did well at school over the following years and went on to university – the first person in my family to do so, as far as anyone knew or could remember. I did see my aunt and uncle occasionally but mostly when they came up to Paisley. We hardly ever went to Millarston and when we did, after my father had bought a car, we usually only visited for a couple of hours and I rarely met any of the village children whom I knew. Often, I would excuse myself from these outings even though I knew it would disappoint my aunt. And, increasingly, I would be out and miss her when she came to our house. She was always far more interested in me than in either of my sisters or any of the other nephews or nieces in the family. My sisters were quite aware of this and rather resented it, quite understandably. I took the attention, and the love, for granted and too seldom bothered to return it.

After university, I moved down to London and started working as a journalist on trade magazines. Later, I scrambled my way into advertising and then television – always chasing more money. I didn't go home very much during those early years. But from time to time, I did find myself thinking about the woman with the bell.

Once I began to wonder about who she was and why she rang that bell, I became steadily more and more puzzled and fascinated. It was only then, seeing her through an adult's eyes rather than a child's, that I truly appreciated just how strange the whole thing was. There was something so vivid and dreamlike about the image of the woman walking round the garden ringing the bell, that I would suddenly 'see' her when I was driving down the motorway to do an interview or some research, or sitting in a script meeting, or lying awake, as I often do, in the middle of the night. I wondered about what might have driven her to behave in that way. No one seemed to make her carry the bell and yet she always did. No one seemed to prevent her walking out of the garden and yet she never even tried, as far as I knew. Sometimes I began to wonder if I hadn't simply imagined, or dreamed, the whole thing.

At family gatherings over the years – weddings, funerals, christenings – I'd seen my aunt and I had asked her once or twice about the woman.

She just shook her head and said she didn't know anything about her. Which I thought was strange, given the way in which she had urged me to stay away from the big house when I was a child. I also tried my mother. She looked at me with an uncharacteristic sharpness and said she knew nothing about any woman or any big house.

My mother has been dead for quite some time now. My aunt died just under a year ago. I went back to Millarston for the funeral, the first time I'd been there in years – I'm ashamed to say that it must have been many, many years.

My uncle was dressed in his best black suit. He took me into the front room where my aunt was laid out in her coffin. She looked tiny. Her hair had gone white and was drawn back from her face in the same severe way that I always remembered. I sat in the front room with her for some time. My uncle didn't cry. He didn't say anything, but kept his eyes on her the whole time we were in the room.

I had meant to go back to Paisley that evening and stay over with my sister. But I ended up sitting with my uncle in the kitchen for most of the night and going straight to the funeral with him the next morning. He had never been a talkative man. But that night he seemed glad to have someone to share his thoughts with, some-one I think (guiltily) who had meant a lot to his wife. He talked about his early life and how he had met her. It was raining outside. And there was a wind getting up. I kept thinking about my aunt, lying in her open coffin in the next room. Doubtless, that was what he was thinking about too. It was at some point that night that I asked him about the woman with the bell.

I was surprised, to say the least, by the story which he told me. I was particularly astonished to learn of the connection – possible, anyway – between myself and the woman. I didn't really believe him – or, rather, I preferred not to believe him. I could see, however, that my uncle was utterly convinced of the truth of what he was saying. I've subsequently checked those facts that can be checked and that side of things holds up pretty well – as far as it goes, anyway. The rest of the story, well – there really is no way of proving it completely one way or the other. You either accept it or you don't.

I'm still not sure quite where I stand myself. But I keep thinking about the look in my uncle's eyes as he talked – especially when he came to the very end of the story, the part which (given that you believe him, of course) directly affected him – and I find that my scepticism is less complete than it was.

Two

In the early 1930s, the state of affairs at the big house was well known in the village and the surrounding area. People no longer talked about it or shook their heads over the way in which the building was going to rack and ruin. No one really bothered now to discuss the strange situation of Nancy Renwick. Nothing had changed for over twenty years and things could well have gone on in exactly the same way for another twenty years or longer if it hadn't been for the arrival of Grace Johnson.

Alec McAuley, the postman, was the first person in the village to lay eyes on Grace Johnson. He was coming back from Renwick House one morning in early October 1934. The figure he saw at first was slight and dark. It was only as he got closer that he realized it was a woman – quite young and attractive at that. She was about a mile away when he first noticed her, walking up towards him, carrying a suitcase in one hand.

McAuley scraped the sole of his boot on the road to bring his bike to a halt and take a good look at her. She was an attractive young woman: far better than just about anything else around here anyway, as he told them in the village bar later that morning. Not much over twenty, he said, and a trim wee thing, too.

'Mornin.' She spoke quietly and smiled at him, shy and awkward. McAuley nodded, studying the battered brown case which she had now put down, as if by simply looking at it he might learn something about her.

'Where ye headed, pet?'

'I was lookin for Renwick House.'

McAuley's eyes came back up to her face. You didn't get many people looking for the big house these days and, of course, you couldn't see it from where they were. It was hidden by the rise of the hill.

'Aye. It's up there. But that's a' that's up there.'

'I was worried I'd got lost.'

He'd thought that himself. In the old days, this road had been a busy one, but not now and not for many years since. He couldn't remember the last time he'd met someone up here.

'What ye goin there for?'

'A job. I heard they needed someone. An I thought they might gie me a start. Even if it was only for a couple of weeks.'

McAuley was surprised by her reply. It was true enough that there was a job going in the big house but he wondered how she knew. The accident had only happened two days before and news still travelled slowly in those times and in that part of the country.

Clair MacIndoe, the maid at the big house, and the cook, Jennie Weir, had been butchering a deer in the kitchen. They had been working separately, talking as they cut and cleaned the joints of meat. Clair MacIndoe was hacking through the bone in a piece of haunch when, presumably because there was a great deal of blood around, or the joint was covered with that slippery white membrane under the skin, from which it had just been separated, the meat had twisted in her grip as she brought the cleaver down.

The heavy, newly-sharpened blade sliced through her hand between thumb and forefinger almost as easily as it would have passed through butter. The knuckles and fingers were still attached to the rest of her hand only by an inch or so of flesh and gristle which the cleaver had missed. It had severed main arteries, shattered the bone and embedded itself in the meat below.

Jennie Weir didn't realize anything was wrong at first and went on working for just a moment or so more. There was no scream, no look of shock on Clair MacIndoe's face, no sign that anything out of the ordinary had happened. It all looked

21

uncannily normal except for the blood pumping from her hand all over the table. But then again there was already so much of the deer's blood on the table and on the stone floor that more would have made no difference, not at first anyway.

Clair slowly pulled her hand away from where it lay on the meat. Her knuckles and fingers gaped at an angle to the rest of her hand. The blood spouted over the silvery, skinned piece of haunch. She looked at Jennie and her mouth opened but she couldn't speak or even make a sound. She began to vomit. Then she fainted. Jennie Weir put a tourniquet on the arm, just above the elbow, and staunched most of the flow of blood. She called her husband who was working in the grounds. He drove the two women to the doctor in the next village. The doctor told them that Jennie Weir had probably saved Clair MacIndoe's life by stopping the blood.

Clair MacIndoe was taken to hospital in Greenock. In the weeks that followed, she contracted septicaemia and came close to death. However, she did survive, although her hand and the lower part of her arm were amputated a month or so after the accident. When the doctors asked her what had actually happened, she was unable to give them any very satisfactory explanation. She said she seemed to be aware of what she was doing but couldn't stop herself.

'Where did ye hear that? Aboot the job?'

'Jist some'dy I met on the road. Why – is it no true?' She seemed genuinely worried at the possibility of this.

'No, it's true enough.'

'They havenae got some'dy else, have they?'

'No as far as I know. I fact, I'm quite certain they've no. No this early.' A glimpse of relief flickered across her face.

'I hope they take me on. I've no been able to get any regular work for a while.'

McAuley nodded. He knew the value of a job and the difficulty of finding one especially at that time, when the yards and factories up in Glasgow were laying off men by the thousands. Even here, in this backwater, they'd get men and sometimes women passing through on their way from Glasgow to the coast, looking for work, prepared to take anything. Of course, in a village as poor as this, with little decent farmland and no hint of twentieth- or even nineteenth-century industry, there was nothing for them.

'Is there any other place I'm likely tae find work if they don't take me on?'

'No round here, pet. No that I know of. An I know most places.'

She shrugged, apparently grateful for his concern, and picked up the case. Its locks gaped open uselessly. A piece of rope, knotted under the handle, kept it shut.

'Fingers crossed, eh?'

'Aye.'

McAuley eased back onto the saddle, ready to push on. He hesitated as if about to say something to her and then changed his mind. She turned back to him, smiling.

'Jist straight on?'

'That's right.'

'Thanks.'

Renwick House was too grand and imposing a building for the elemental landscape around it, hills and moorland which had hardly changed for thousands of years. It was striving to create an effect, to make a statement about the wealth and self-importance of the people who had built it; while everything else around it just was as nature had intended it to be.

By the time the girl arrived, many years after there had been any real money in the family, the house's pretensions had been exposed even further by years of neglect. The wind and the rain swept in off the sea, day after day, blackening the stone and punishing the fabric of the building. Slates had been torn from the roof. The rain battered ceaselessly at the woodwork and worked its way in through tiny cracks and gaps that grew steadily wider and deeper as the years passed. The stonework was still reasonably sound but that, too, was beginning to succumb to the effects of time.

There had been a very attractive, much smaller, laird's house on the same site in the eighteenth century. This had been knocked down and replaced in the 1850s when the money which the Renwicks had first made from astute canal-building speculation was paying large dividends after being reinvested in land and factories. This high tide of wealth and prosperity quickly ebbed away again towards the turn of the century. In the second half of the nineteenth century, the house and, more especially, the gardens had been famous and were regularly visited and written about by many people. They were, according to one Victorian gardening author, 'the finest gardens anywhere in the West of Scotland and for many miles beyond'.

There was a superb wild area on the bank between the ridge and the house. In early summer, this would be sprinkled with the reds and blues of poppies and irises embedded deep in the long grass. There was a remarkable collection of rhododendrons, most grown from seed or cuttings shipped from the mountains of China and Tibet and otherwise unknown in this country. There was also a fine display of camellias in the glasshouse that ran along the south-western side of the building. But it was the walled garden that drew so many compliments and so much admiring attention. The wall was eight feet high and several feet thick. It enclosed an area of just under an acre. The shelter of the ridge and this wall helped to create a garden of surprising lushness and colour. Here, in season, there were large and joyous displays of white and pink dahlias. There were deep blue delphiniums which reached almost to the top of the wall. One stretch of this wall, perhaps thirty feet long, was given over to a ceanothus which drooped its long blue brushes of flower in profusion in May and June. There was a pond where water lilies covered the surface in late summer. Close up against the south-facing wall, there were several peach trees all of which bore fruit, though not always in great abundance. More than one commentator wrote, or hinted, that there was almost something unsettling in the intensity and lushness of the garden in an area that is normally so unsuited, even hostile, to the gardener's art.

For many years now, though, there had been no visitors. There was simply nothing for them to see. The walled garden was badly neglected. The rhododendrons were still there but hopelessly overgrown and many of the finer specimens had been lost. There were no camellias. The skeleton of the glasshouse still existed but most of its glass had gone. The putty had dried and cracked so that the panes sat in their frames, until a gust of wind would lift them out and shatter them on the ground which was now littered with splinters of glass that no one, not even Simmie Weir, the gardener, had bothered to clear away.

Mrs Weir, the cook and housekeeper, was in the front drawing-room when her eye was caught by the figure on the road. This room was still in reasonable condition and Mrs Weir did her best to keep it up. With its highly polished wooden floor, richly patterned Indian carpet and pale blue velvet furniture, it was a reminder of how things had once been.

She watched the girl for some time, wondering who she was and why she was coming here. Mrs Weir, too, assumed she must be lost and was going to have to carry that case all the way back.

Mrs Weir was a heavy, quietly spoken woman in her early fifties. She'd long since learned to expect little from life and to be ready to lose even that at a moment's notice. She'd given birth to five children, but only three were still alive: two in Australia and one in London, which came to much the same thing in terms of seeing them, as she herself said. She and her husband, Simmie, had moved down from Glasgow eleven years ago. Simmie had lost his job in the Bridgeton steel-works and been out of work for over a year. They had heard about this place through a relative who lived near the village. There was no local couple who could take over the running of the house – or, perhaps, who wanted to – so the position was theirs for the asking. Mrs Weir looked after the house and Simmie took care of the gardens as best he could.

Mrs Weir had expected the girl to turn back when she found out that the road ended at the house. But she came right up to the door, set down her case and knocked.

Mrs Weir made her way through the dark hall and opened the door.

'I'm lookin for a job. I heard you might need some'dy.'

There was an innocence about the girl that instantly dispelled any of the wariness that is natural in country people towards strangers. Even so, she was as surprised at the mention of the job as McAuley had been, if not more so. The shock of the accident with Clair MacIndoe was still fresh in her mind and this sudden reference to it by a stranger brought it all vividly back to her just as she was beginning to forget it.

'Where d'ye hear that?'

'Some'dy I met on the road.'

'Who?'

'I don't know his name. He jist said there might be a job goin up here.'

Mrs Weir looked at her for a moment. There was something oddly familiar about the girl, as if she had seen her somewhere before, though she couldn't have said where. Mrs Weir pushed the door open a little more and nodded noncommittally.

'Come on through tae the kitchen.'

Mrs Weir led the girl through the shabby hall into the kitchen. She nodded for her to sit down at the table and went over to the range to attend to a pot of soup that was rattling its lid. A big black cast iron range with oven, hotplates and open fire took up most of one wall. There was a sink by the window, looking out onto the garden. The other walls were taken up with well-scrubbed wooden cupboards and shelves for pots and dishes. The floor was stone slabs worn smooth and hollowed out here and there by the passage of many feet over many years.

Mrs Weir stirred the soup and edged the pot off the hotplate. When she was satisfied with the way it was cooking, she turned back to the girl, wiping her hands with her apron.

'Ye must be tired.'

'I'm fine.'

'Been on the road long?'

'Aye.'

'Where d'ye start from this mornin?'

'A village nearer the coast. I cannae mind what it wis called.'

'Dalry?'

'Aye, maybe.' There was a slight pause. This seemed to make the girl nervous.

'I've got references.'

'What's yir name?'

'Grace Johnson.'

'What ye doing around these parts?'

'I've jist done the summer in a big hotel near Skelmorlie. I was makin my way up to Glasgow, lookin for work wherever I can find it. There's no much around.'

'Ye might do better jist goin straight on tae Glasgow.'

'Work's no easier to find there than anywhere else these days.'

'I suppose ye're right.'

The girl had been undoing the rope around her case as they talked. She lifted the lid and took out an envelope that had been carefully placed on top. Mrs Weir was pleased to see that the clothes inside were neatly folded, all ironed and cleaned. The girl handed over the envelope, which was unsealed.

'This is my letter of reference. Ye can write tae the manager if ye like. Or phone him.'

'There's nae phone here.'

The girl nodded, still clearly anxious, as Mrs Weir took out and read the letter. It spoke warmly of the girl, saying that she was reliable, efficient and trustworthy. It was neatly typed on the hotel's headed notepaper and signed by the manager.

This was more than Mrs Weir could have hoped for. The girl looked trim and tidy, someone who'd do a good job, someone she wouldn't mind having around the house. As far as she was concerned, Grace Johnson was a godsend. She couldn't run this house on her own and she was delighted, if a little surprised, to get someone who seemed so good so quickly, out of the blue like this.

'I don't decide about these things ye understand. That would be up to the Master. I'll go and huv a word wi him.'

A Child of Air

Mrs Weir was gone for about five minutes. When she returned, she asked the girl to come with her. They went back into the hall and turned up the wide wooden stairs. The runner on the stairs was an old Persian rug, the colours muted with age and wear but still beautiful – intricate and almost strangely sensual in a house where everything seemed to be dark, hard, joyless. The walls were covered with heavy green wallpaper which, here and there, was torn or had begun to peel. There were paintings on the walls. Some were portraits, not particularly good, of previous members of the family. Others were of the canals in which the family had invested. These were odd, curiously attractive paintings, usually of a barge being pulled by a horse and carter across an agricultural or industrial landscape, full of smoke-belching chimneys. Even though they were pictures of motion, they were curiously stiff and stilted, as if nothing in them had ever moved or ever would. (You can still see several of these paintings hanging in Paisley Museum and they apparently have several more in store. They were bequeathed to the museum by the trustees of the estate when the house was finally demolished in the mid sixties.)

On one side of the hall, a short corridor led into the drawing-room. On the other side, where there should have been a corresponding corridor, and a correspondingly large dining-room or second drawing-room, there was simply a pair of heavy black curtains drawn closely together. The girl looked at these but Mrs Weir thought she would say nothing about this for the time being. She'd leave that to the Master. Or the girl could find out for herself.

On the half-landing, there was a large stained glass window. It was intricately and delicately patterned but, because of the ridge and the trees behind the house, this window was never seen to its best advantage and only served to make the hall darker. The two women followed the stairs up to the first landing and went to the left along a corridor at the end of which stood a door. Mrs Weir knocked. There was a muffled response from inside. Mrs Weir opened the door and went in, beckoning the girl to follow.

The room was a study, remarkably well ordered, with bookshelves from floor to ceiling on most of the walls. There was a fire burning in the grate but this was more for the benefit of the books (to keep the damp at bay) than for that of the occupant. The warmth and the stale air and the way in which the books surrounded you could make the room seem like the nest, or den, of some large insect or beetle – that was how Simmie Weir felt about it whenever he had to go up there, which was as infrequently as he could manage.

James Renwick looked up from the desk. His eyes went straight to the girl. He was in his forties, a strong and still vigorous man several inches over six feet. His face was brown from the

time he spent in the fields, working the few acres
the house still kept up. His eyes were as dark as
his hair – or his heart, as some of the villagers
would have said, though never within his hearing.

'This is the girl I told ye about, Sir. Her name is
Grace Johnson.'

'Mrs Weir says ye've got a letter of reference.'
She handed him the letter. He read it in silence.

'The wage is three pounds a month. I trust that
will be acceptable to ye.'

'Aye, Sir.' He handed her back the letter.

'Very well. We'll see how ye do.'

'Thank you, Sir.'

'Mrs Weir will tell ye what to do. At a' times, ye
do exactly as she says. If and when the other maid
returns, ye'll go. Is that quite clear?'

'Sir.'

Renwick glanced at Mrs Weir. There was clearly
some kind of question being asked of her, even
though not a word had been spoken. Mrs Weir
responded by shaking her head very slightly.

'There is one thing I should mention. There's
only myself and my sister in the house now. My
sister lives downstairs in her own part of the
house. Ye are at no time to attempt to see her or
speak to her. D'ye understand that?'

'Aye, Sir.'

'Every afternoon at five she goes out to the
garden. Make sure ye're inside at that time, every
day. Is that clear?'

'Sir.'

'Ye are in no danger from my sister. And ye are tae pay no attention to her. What my sister does is her concern, no yours.'

The girl nodded. He looked at her again. it was as if something about her puzzled him.

'Ye're no frae the village?'

She shook her head. 'No, Sir.'

'I thought maybe I'd seen ye before.' The girl said nothing. She waited to be dismissed, which Renwick did with a brief nod as he went back to making notes from the book which he'd been reading.

Mrs Weir took her up to the top floor. This was where the house showed its neglect most clearly. There was a narrow central corridor with bare boards. The walls were stained where the rain had seeped in from above. Mrs Weir showed the girl into a small room that looked out over the front of the house to the moor and the hills beyond. There were clothes and various personal items scattered around the room, as if someone – slightly untidy – had just walked out of the room.

'This was the ither maid's room. I don't know how ye feel aboot stayin here but it's the only decent room. It's no sae damp and I think ye'll be mair comfortable in here.'

'It's fine.'

Grace opened the window, letting a gust of air whistle into the room and disturb the curtains. Several of the photographs that Clair MacIndoe had left in front of the small dressing table mirror fluttered to the floor. Mrs Weir picked them up and put them into one of the drawers.

'Where do you sleep?'

Mrs Weir at first thought this an odd question. But then she realized that the girl was probably just a little frightened and wanted to know that someone was close by.

'Simmie, my husband, and me, we've got the wee cottage round the side of the house. We're never far away.'

The girl smiled, seemingly reassured by this.

'You get yirself settled in. Then come downstairs and we'll get ye startet.'

They were in the kitchen, Mrs Weir kneading dough, Grace scraping vegetables at the sink, when they first heard the bell.

The girl stopped and looked over at Mrs Weir.

'That's the Mistress, like he said.'

The bell rang out again. Mrs Weir wondered if she should have said a bit more to the girl but it was rather late for that now. Her main anxiety was that the girl might leave as abruptly as she'd come. They were so much on their own here and there was nothing else for her. They could wake up in the morning and find her gone: that had happened several times with other maids before they'd found Clair MacIndoe. On the whole, Mrs Weir had thought it best to let the girl see for herself and get used to it as she had done. If she

was going to leave, there was nothing Mrs Weir
could do to stop her.

The kitchen was a half-basement. The girl had
to lean forward, over the sink, and look up to see
anything of the garden. Mrs Weir was relieved to
notice that she seemed curious, and almost surprisingly undisturbed, by her first sight of Nancy
Renwick. The woman crossed directly in front of
the window, ringing the bell as she went, her
footsteps crunching on the gravel path. She wore
a dark red coat with a hood, so that Grace couldn't
see her face clearly.

'What's wrong wi her?'

Mrs Weir didn't answer the question directly:
she could get round to that in its own good time
when – if – the girl settled in.

'She's been like that for a long time. Long afore
I came here.'

Nancy Renwick turned as she came to the high
brick wall that ran round this inner garden. She
walked up the path, away from the house, ignor-
ing the doorway that would have led her out onto
open moorland.

'Where's she goin?'

'Up the garden. She never goes ootside.'

'Why the bell? Does she have to ring that?'

'No. No really . . .'

Mrs Weir had chosen to answer the second
question rather than the first; and, as the first was
not repeated, she was content to let things lie for
the time being. Grace went back to scraping the

carrots. She still looked out of the window from time to time. Even when Nancy Renwick was out of sight, and all they could hear was the sound of the bell tolling out across the garden, she'd look up occasionally. But she didn't ask any more questions, not that afternoon anyway.

Nancy Renwick walked to the part of the garden furthest from the house and took a seat in the old summer house. The bell went on ringing. Mrs Weir chatted to the girl, asking her a little about herself and the place she'd just been working in. Grace seemed reluctant to say very much. Mrs Weir could understand that: the girl had just arrived here, she'd need a little time to find her feet. Mrs Weir had already taken to her. She didn't know much about her but she felt comfortable in her presence. She found she could talk to her more easily than she had ever spoken to Clair MacIndoe: there had always been a rivalry between the two women, a clear demarcation of territory and duties, which were fiercely defended on both sides. Now Mrs Weir found, as quite often afterwards, that she was doing most of the talking. She talked about her children and how they'd gone off and started to raise their own families, which she might never see. The girl seemed interested, which no doubt helped to reinforce the affection which Mrs Weir already felt for her. As they talked, they could hear the bell ringing out from the garden.

After twenty or so minutes, Nancy Renwick left

the summer house and continued to follow the path round the walled garden. This brought her back to the house. Grace stopped working again as the woman crossed in front of the window above her. Mrs Weir was in the middle of a story about her eldest daughter's son having an accident on the ship that took them to Australia.

'Are ye all right?'

'I'm fine.'

'Ye don't need tae worry about her. I know it's a bit strange but really—'

The girl nodded. Mrs Weir smiled, relieved, and went back to her story. They heard the woman climb some steps, just to one side of the kitchen window. A door closed.

Only then, finally, did the bell stop.

Three

The alarm woke James Renwick at six o'clock. It was still dark. He switched on the bedside light and dressed quickly. He had shaved the night before. All his clothes were laid out ready on the armchair by the fire. The fire had gone out long ago but he could still feel some warmth from it on his skin.

He picked up an old leather satchel from the side of the armchair. It was creased and cracked with years of use. The worst tears, and some of the seams, had been stitched over. One of the buckles had been lost and the other was held in place by only the thinnest remnant of leather. He took his bible from the bedside table and put it inside the satchel. He switched out the light and went out of the room.

Renwick's bedroom was on the first floor, opposite his study. He walked quickly along the

41

hall without switching on the light. There was a little brightness thrown into the house by the moon but he knew his way around so well that he could have found his way downstairs without a light even on the blackest of nights. He made very little noise as he came along the hall and down the stairs.

The car was waiting for him outside. Simmie would, as usual, have filled it with petrol and driven it round to the front of the house on Saturday evening. It was a long black Austin, about six years old. Simmie had left the keys in the lock. At the first attempt, the engine turned over but didn't catch. He tried again. It croaked into life.

There was no hint of dawn yet. He kept the headlights on and let the car glide down the hill, sometimes startling a rabbit or an owl.

He passed through the silent, sleeping village and stopped at the junction with the main road. He turned east, heading initially towards Glasgow. Light was beginning to seep into the sky as if some great lid was being slowly prised off the top of the world. After a few miles, he switched off the headlights, now driving directly into the angry red eye of the sun.

Renwick arrived in Leith just before midday. The docks were quieter than they would have been during the week but there were still a few ships loading and unloading. He drove past the docks and then turned away from the sea again and went back among grimy side streets which were mostly tenements or cramped terraced houses. The hall he was preaching in was a small solid building in a street which was mostly warehouses or small factories. There was a printing works beside the hall. All of the other buildings in the street were quiet.

He was met by one of the elders, Jack Cunningham, a small red-faced man well into his sixties, who took him through to a back room with a toilet and wash basin. Renwick bathed his face and changed his collar. The old man brought him some soup and bread and then left him alone.

After he had eaten, Renwick sat on one of the hard benches that ran round the room and rested. He closed his eyes but didn't go to sleep. He could have lain down and possibly slept but that would have been wrong in his eyes. This had been a long but not especially difficult journey. Sometimes he went much further, up to Montrose or down into the Borders or even the north of England. The hardness of the journey was somehow part of the task, almost as important as the sermon he would deliver. Occasionally he would preach nearer home, in Glasgow or Greenock, but that was too easy and, though he was sometimes tempted to concentrate on these places, he never gave in to the temptation. Indeed, he would actively push himself to seek places that involved a long and tiring journey. He could never allow himself to take the easier option. That was weak. Only by suffering, only by pushing yourself to the limits, could you be sure you were doing the right thing.

The places in which he preached were not ordinary churches. They were small secessionist chapels, tabernacles or mission halls. They adhered to a fierce and extreme form of protestantism. These small churches were usually democratic to a fault, as the Covenanters had been. They tended to recognize no other authority than that of God. So they had no ministers. Some even had no elders or any structure of authority within the sect. Each member of the congregation was equal with every other in the sight of God and therefore in the lesser sight of each other. They would take it in turns to preach or they would invite lay preachers, such as Renwick, to minister to them from time to time. They tended to see the world in very simple terms, dictated almost entirely by an absolute belief in everything in the bible. Their world view was as simple and narrow as Renwick's – they believed in God and the bible and very little else. If you had God and the bible, what else did you need?

Renwick, unlike most other lay preachers, had been to university and studied divinity with a view to taking up a ministry within the Church of Scotland. However, although in some ways a brilliant student and certainly a passionate and strong preacher, he lacked other qualities that would have made him a good choice as minister. He had an arrogance and an inability to mix easily with ordinary people, to offer them comfort, and to reconcile them to their lives, all of which arguably are more important in the everyday duties of a minister than the power of making sermons or constructing elegant analytical arguments from scripture.

Renwick was one of the last students of his year to be offered a position and when it came, it was with a benign, vague old minister in a poor parish on the outskirts of Motherwell. Many of the men worked in the steelworks. Some were socialists and communists and, though not openly contemptuous of him or the authority of the Church, saw no place in their world for religion.

Renwick was no more at ease with the wives and children who largely made up the congregation each Sunday than he was with the men. The old minister felt he might mellow in the welter of human difficulties and suffering he would encounter among these poor, badly nourished, literally hopeless families. But, in fact, the opposite happened. Renwick seemed to harden against the congregation and alienate them even further. The old man found himself made uneasy and unwell by the strain of dealing with Renwick, who couldn't see the world in terms of small defeats and equally small victories, but only in terms of ultimate salvation. Something that the old man had long ago ceased to worry about, though still quite secure in his faith.

The old man became ill and retired two years after Renwick went to his parish. Renwick assumed he would be allowed to take over but a new minister was appointed over him and the new incumbent specifically requested his own choice of assistant. He didn't say so but he, and the Kirk Session, felt that Renwick had actually come between the people and the Church. They assured him they would find him another position but Renwick, his pride stung, had already turned his back on them and withdrawn from the Church.

He moved back to Millarston. His father, from whom he had taken his religion, assured him that the fault lay not with him but with those who knew not the true ways of the Lord. The father, Old John Renwick, had fostered Renwick's fierce, joyless, unforgiving brand of religion. It had been passed on to him by his father, like some hereditary disease that would ravage the lives not only of the present generation but of succeeding generations too.

John Renwick had tried to get James the incumbency at the village when the minister retired a few years later. The church in the village had been built by the Renwicks and the family had chosen the minister for over a century. But the Church authorities had been discouraging for many years these private powers of patronage over a specific church and, in James's case, they were particularly opposed to it. They felt he was not ready – perhaps never would be – to take over a ministry. A new minister, a fairly young man called Hebden, was brought in and had been there now for over fifteen years.

From the moment the new minister was appointed, no Renwick ever set foot in the church they had built. There were some people in the village who said that this defeat had broken the old man. It was the first time his will had ever been seriously and publicly challenged. He lived on for another four years or so but people said he was never the same again. Certainly, he became less of a force in the lives of the villagers.

Renwick became totally isolated from the life of the village. He interpreted his rejection not as an indication that he was in any way wrong but that he was right and he knew how you must suffer for what is right: the more you suffer, the more right you must be. He worked on the few acres of land that were still capable of growing something. He did this like any village labourer, 'beasting into it' as the men would say, harder than any of them would have done. In the evenings, and when there was nothing to do on the land, he'd work on his sermons or his history of the Covenanters, many of whom had come from this part of the country. On Sundays, he would preach. That was the pattern of his life and had been for over twenty years.

Renwick was to preach at three. Cunningham came through for him a few minutes before the hour. He followed the old man out of the back room and along the corridor with its framed black and white photographs of biblical sites in Palestine.

The hall was full but it was actually quite small and there were probably no more than sixty or seventy people in all. They were dressed in their best: dark colours, often black. There had been some talk in the hall but this died away as the two men entered.

There was a low platform at the front with three steps leading up to it, cut into the platform at the side. Renwick took his place on a seat at the back. The older man stood at the front.

'Good afternoon, fellow Brothers and Sisters in Christ. I welcome you to our meeting where we can worship in the true faith and demonstrate to the Lord on high our feelings for Him.'

From the congregation, there came several muted cries of 'Hallelujah' and 'Amen'.

'Today, we are privileged to have with us Brother James Renwick to assist us in our worship of God and further understanding of His word as laid out in the Gospels. Many of ye will already know Brother Renwick as a strong and a shinin beacon of the true faith, as a man who's as well acquainted wi the Gospels as onybody here and wi the ways o the Lord. Amen!'

A chorus of voices, stronger now, echoed this

around the hall. Renwick sat quite still throughout. The old man waited until the noise had died down.

'We will begin our service by singin Psalm 68.'

The tiny congregation rose to its feet, as did Renwick. They sang loudly, filling the little hall with voices.

> 'Let God arise, and scattered
> let all his enemies be;
> And let all those that do him hate
> before his presence flee.
> As smoke is driv'n, so drive thou them:
> As fire melts wax away,
> Before God's face let wicked men
> so perish and decay.'

They were poor people by and large. Most were working men with their wives and families – painters, carpenters, electricians and engineers. A few owned shops or small businesses but they were only slightly better off than the workers. They were not the very poorest, mostly, but few of them had ever owned much in their lives or ever would.

After the first psalm, the elder gave the news of what had happened within their congregation and outside. There was another psalm. A prayer. The elder spoke on the text, 'He that is faithful in that which is least is faithful also in much' from Luke 16, 10. The collection was taken. After this Renwick rose and began to speak. He held onto

49

the edges of the lectern, white-knuckled, through-out his sermon.

'The text today is "For where two or three are gathered together in my name, there am I in the midst of them".'

His eyes took them in, searching over the small congregation as if trying to read their hearts. One or two voices shouted out 'Hallelujah'. As he waited, the door at the back of the hall opened and a young woman in a black coat and wearing a black bonnet entered and took a seat on the bench nearest her. Renwick looked at her for a moment but couldn't really see her and no one else in the hall paid her any attention. They seemed not even to have noticed the door opening. When he began again, his voice had more attack, more passion, as if he could feel the congregation responding to him, willing him to greater effort.

'This is the charter of Christian brotherhood and equality. When the Lord spake these words, He gave to every band, however small, of His followers, who might at any future time fore-gather to worship Him, their inalienable law.'

The voices from the congregation were coming back to him more loudly now and more fre-quently, setting a very definite rhythm that would work its way slowly and inexorably towards its climax.

'He did not – nay, He did not, I say – place their right in the keeping of any presbytery or synod. Nor did He give control or supervision into the hands of any bishop or priest whatsoever. His charter is divine and gives its duties and privileges tae each gatherin of worshippers without intervention of council. It is given direct from Himself. It brings the promise of His ain presence whenever and wherever it is asked in humility and sincerity. Aye, indeed!' This was a shout, echoed round the room. Renwick's voice dropped again, having worked to one small climax he would begin to make his way towards a second, higher climax and then a third and a fourth and so on. He looked again at the young woman on the last bench. Her head was still bowed. Something about her disturbed him slightly but he pushed on.

'There is nae limitin in this respect. Nothin is said to indicate whit forms should be used. Gathered in my name – that's a'.'

He spoke for over forty minutes, examining the text from every side. He railed against the structures that men had reared in God's name, when their purpose was clearly to glorify themselves rather than God. He cursed the church of Rome for its wanton displays of pomp and ceremony – anathema, he was certain, in the eyes of God. He argued back from the bible showing how there was no justification for creating these grand places and structures of worship. There was 'no whisper from the Lord's lips' to justify those who would seek to control any band of worshippers that ever gathered in His name. He moved on to show, again from scripture, how those who seeked to usurp Christ's ministry would be damned to Hell. And he urged them to consider the pains of Hell and of a life with the eternal absence of God. And then slowly, carefully, he brought his audience back down, his voice now quieter, the ideas and thoughts he now expressed designed to confirm them in their own view of the way forward, and of their own rightness in the eyes of God, if not of the world. Regularly, throughout this, his eyes came back to the young woman in the black bonnet. He had no idea why. He just found himself looking at her again and again.

'The errors of the past are for our instruction. We are not to huv sympathy with error merely because of its age. Nor accept any doctrine from the most learned or respected of our friends merely because synods huv said so.'

'Amen. Amen,' chorused the now almost exhausted voices from the congregation.

'We recognize nae authority but God's ain word. Nae church law but His. Nae orders but His. Nae word but His. We will always – always, I say again – receive the teachings of the Lord in preference to anything said by men. Praise the Lord. Amen.'

Renwick sat down, utterly exhausted. The sweat was running from his forehead and he mopped it away with a handkerchief. As he drew the cloth across his eyes, the young woman on the last bench rose and he caught a brief glimpse of her face. She smiled directly at him and then turned and slipped out the door. Again, no one seemed to notice her leaving. He shook his head and wiped the sweat from his eyes again. He was puzzled. She had looked uncannily like the girl from the house, although it was of course impossible that it could have been her. The congregation sang one last hymn, joined in prayer again and then dispersed.

Renwick returned to the back room. He was brought a cup of tea by one of the women. Several of the elders joined him and congratulated him on his sermon. One took him to task on his interpretation of one of his texts but seemed satisfied with Renwick's answer. There was then a short session when any of the congregation who wanted something in the scriptures explained would come to Renwick. He could usually recall the exact text, and its context, without referring to the Bible and would instantly offer a gloss on the passage that was reasoned, clear and satisfying.

That same Sunday, Grace's first in the house, Mrs Weir asked her to join her and Simmie for lunch in their cottage. She'd only rarely extended this invitation to Clair MacIndoe. On those few occasions, Mrs Weir was never very sure whether they were putting up with Clair, or she was putting up with them. Clair seemed to grind her teeth and get through these events with about as little pleasure and enjoyment as Simmie.

The Weirs' small, white-washed cottage was built against the outside of the wall that ran round the garden and it faced away from the big house, with an uninterrupted and breathtaking view of the moors and the hills – the only good thing about living there, as Simmie would say.

The girl came over about eleven in the morning and helped Mrs Weir prepare lunch. Simmie was less sure about her than his wife. It didn't make sense to him that she would choose to work here. Mrs Weir would admit, with a sigh, that she doubted the girl would stay long. She'd be sad to see her go but she would understand. There was just nothing for the girl here. Nothing.

Simmie knew that Grace worked well and took some of the burden of running the place off his wife's shoulders. But there was something about the girl that made him uncomfortable. He couldn't put this into words and, after a few attempts, gave up trying: his wife was happy enough with her – that was all that mattered.

In the afternoon, Mrs Weir and Grace took a walk round the garden. It was an unusually mild day for October. They spent some time in the old summer house – Mrs Weir doing most of the talking. Later, the wind came up and they moved on, ending up at Simmie's greenhouse. This was also Simmie's bothy, his own private retreat, where he spent much time on his own, working with the plants or just smoking his pipe. Even

Mrs Weir rarely entered it and when she did it was always rather tentatively, as if this was a part of her husband's life over which she had no claim.

Simmie had just picked up a paper packet of seeds and tipped the contents, hard little purple balls, into the palm of his hand. Grace asked,

'Whit's that?'

'Bird of Paradise. I've tried them three times an got absolutely nothin fae them. This is whit they should look like.'

He put the seeds back into the packet and reached up for one of the books he kept on a shelf above the bench.

Opening it, he showed her a highly coloured photograph of a spectacular cluster of orange and purple flowers.

'Maybe you jist huvnae got the touch.'

'An you dae?'

The girl smiled at Simmie, almost – he thought – taunting or challenging him.

'A'right,' said Simmie, 'let's see whit ye can dae.'

'I'm away back inside tae get the tea on. Don't be too long.' Mrs Weir was pleased that Simmie appeared to be softening a little towards the girl. He took a few handfuls from the big hundredweight jute sacks he kept under his bench: one of gravel, one of sand for every two of soil. He piled these like an alchemist one on top of the other and began to knead the mixture together, turning it between his fingers and letting it fall from his hands until it took on a consistency of colour and texture that satisfied him.

He lifted a six-inch clay pot from a stack by the window, put some stones in the base and then filled it with the mixture in front of him. He packed down the compost with his fingers.

'How many d'ye want tae try?'

'Jist the one.'

Grace poured the seeds from the packet into the palm of her left hand. She looked at them for a moment and then pinched one out. She emptied the rest of them onto a sheet of greaseproof paper which Simmie had spread on the workbench for her. She placed the seed in the pot and covered it lightly with soil. Then she blew onto it.

'A special wee bit of magic.' Simmie shook his head, indulging her. He was still unsure what it was about her that he disliked. Maybe he was just being unreasonable. Not at all an unusual occurrence, as his wife would have said.

'Where does it go?' He showed her a shelf in the end section of the greenhouse which he kept at a steady warm temperature all the year round. She placed the pot in the corner. This was all done with a childlike enthusiasm and attention to detail which he found quite engaging. Maybe he would get to like her after all.

She went off to help Mrs Weir. He potted up eleven more seeds with the same mixture and placed them on the same shelf. Then he washed his hands and joined the women.

After a few weeks, Grace's seed had sprouted. He repotted it into a much larger pot, out of a guarded curiosity, and then left it alone. It flowered several months later – the only Bird of Paradise that ever flowered in that greenhouse.

Renwick came into Glasgow at about nine-thirty that night.

He hated this long dull road that swept in from the east. It was mile after mile of shabby poverty, dark tenements rising up on either side of the road, closing out any view of the sky or the hills to the south and north of the city.

There were few people around at this time on a Sunday night but those whom he saw were poor, undernourished and badly dressed. If they were children, they often had no shoes and what clothes they did wear were inappropriate for a cold October evening. If they were men, they were generally drunks making their erratic way home with heads lolling and fingers constantly feeling for the support of a tenement wall or a lamp post. He had no idea where they would find drink on a Sunday night but he supposed there were always places, always ways.

He drove along by the docks on the north side of the river. At Anderston Quay, he turned up Cheapside Street – a dark sidestreet of warehouses and shipping offices. About halfway up, he pulled into the side and stopped the car. He didn't get out, nor turn off the engine. He sat there for a few moments, watching the three women who stood at the entrance of the cobbled alley that cut across into Whitehall Street. There were two young ones and an older one, in her forties.

The three women talked quietly. They would fall silent for a moment or so, scanning the street. Then they would talk and laugh again. A man – he looked like a foreign sailor – came along, spoke to one of the younger women for a moment and left with her.

Renwick was very careful, most of the time, to split this part of his life off from the village and the house. But then his whole life was a case of splitting things off, of seeing things only in the way that they should be seen – whatever the cost. He had made strenuous efforts never to touch or become involved with the women in the house or the village. But these efforts were not always successful. Occasionally, even while his father was alive, he had slept with some of the women servants and he had more recently developed a relationship of sorts with Clair MacIndoe. He would appear in her room at night, quite abruptly, without even knocking on the door. He would climb into her bed and, with no preliminaries and not a word spoken, make love to her – though that hardly seems the phrase to use. It's difficult to see what a woman could get from such a relationship or why she would allow it to continue without complaining, without demanding something in return, but for whatever reason – whether she was afraid to lose her job or because some love (no matter how little) was better than none – she did permit it to run on in its own sporadic, explosive, one-sided way.

Renwick sat in the car, wanting to drive away. But he also wanted the older woman, to take whatever comfort he could find in her body – no matter how brief or expensively purchased in terms of guilt and self-recrimination.

The older woman looked directly over at him.

Her coat lay open. He could see the shape of her breasts and her belly under the brown shimmering material of her dress. It was relatively short, showing her legs to just below the knee. She stood with her legs slightly apart, deliberately, provocatively.

His hand reached for the gear shift. He clicked the cold metal rod into first. He started to drive off but changed his mind almost instantly.

He drew back into the kerb.

When he went over to the older woman, she smiled and walked off with him, glad that she would earn at least some money tonight.

Four

It was quite soon after the girl arrived that Mrs Weir told her Nancy Renwick's story.

Nancy had just come into the garden, ringing the bell as usual. Mrs Weir and Grace were making bramble jam in the kitchen. The girl carried on with her work – scrubbing out and drying the large two pound jars Mrs Weir used and then cutting out seals for the jars from greaseproof paper. Every so often, though, she'd look out at the garden.

Mrs Weir was surprised that the girl hadn't asked any questions. It wasn't as if she wasn't interested in Nancy: her eyes were on her all the time she was outside. But then that was understandable. It must seem a strange sight if you hadn't got so used to it over the last seven years that you hardly thought about it any more.

Mrs Weir wondered about holding off for a

while but decided, as she watched Grace looking out into the garden, even though Nancy Renwick was out of sight, that this was as good a moment as any. Besides, Grace hadn't been down to the village or into Lochwinnoch yet. If she stayed, as looked more and more likely now, she'd get talking to some of the villagers and someone was bound to mention Nancy. They talked a lot of nonsense about Nancy in the village and Mrs Weir didn't want Grace hearing any of that before she'd told her the truth.

Mrs Weir started her story while Nancy was out in the garden and was still talking long after Nancy had gone back inside and the bell had fallen silent again.

In the years before the First World War, Old John Renwick was the head of the family. He was a strict authoritarian figure, still exercising to the full the power that he felt was his by rights over the lives of his own family and the people who lived on his lands. He was a fiercely, darkly, religious man. Despite the efforts of the Church authorities in Edinburgh, he had retained, like his father before him, the power to choose the minister for the village and surrounding parish and this was not a burden he shirked. The ministers in his time were fire and brimstone characters whose voices thundered out over the congregation of the little church, sometimes eloquently, sometimes less so, like shells fired in battle – but then that, after all, was how Old Renwick and the ministers and many of the villagers saw life: as a struggle to the death with the forces of evil that were as real and as physical and as devious as any human enemy.

Old John Renwick would sit in church, listening grimly. His wife – in many ways worse than him – was always beside him. The two children would sit on the other side of their mother, silent, not daring to move throughout the long wearying services. John Renwick would know at a glance who was there each Sunday morning and who was not, who had a good reason for being absent and who did not. There were precious few good reasons for being absent in his eyes other than death – and even then, the villagers said, he was unlikely to let it go unless you'd been dead a good few days and had gone well stiff.

They could, and did, joke about him when they were well out of his hearing but few of them defied him over churchgoing, or anything else, for long. They would be at the church whether they liked it or not and they would do most of the other things that he wanted, too. He was used to obedience, in all things and on all points. It wasn't something he insisted on loudly. He didn't need to do that. It was simply his. By rights. A quality of his being, just as the grass was green. That was the way this particular little part of the universe was ordered.

This was why, when the business with his

daughter happened, he had no doubts – ever – that he had done the right thing. Doubt had no place in his world.

When she was seventeen, Nancy Renwick had become fond of a young man called Robin Wilson. She had known him since she was a child as he lived not far from the big house. Somehow, at this point in her life, they had begun to spend much of their time together. They would go for walks together. Talk together. When Old Renwick heard about this, he forbade Nancy to see Wilson again.

Wilson wasn't good enough for her. His family had no land of their own, only what they rented from Renwick. There was also a sense in which Renwick was shocked by the sudden emergence of even such innocent sexuality in his daughter but this, of course, was not something he would ever have admitted to anyone, even his wife, perhaps even himself. And so the proclamation was made, in the study, one dark October afternoon: she was to see Wilson no more. And that, as he thought, was the end of it.

As you might expect, Nancy and Wilson continued to meet in secret. Wilson was no older, more knowing, seducer. He was, in his own way, as innocent as Nancy. Inevitably, given the intensity which their relationship now took on, they became lovers. Equally inevitably, given their ignorance, it was not long before she became pregnant.

Subsequent events followed a fairly predictable

pattern – up to a point, anyway. Nancy and Wilson tried to conceal the pregnancy for as long as possible. They made plans to run away together and indeed this is what they did. But they had little money and were easily found in Glasgow a few days after they had left. Wilson was given a sizeable amount of money on the condition that he leave that day for Australia: if he didn't accept his family would be turned out of their house and thrown off their land.

He did go but returned to Scotland, though not the village, a few years later. During the War, he joined the Army and died, very soon after, in Flanders. Nancy was brought back to the big house. She was not allowed to go outside. As soon as the baby emerged into the world, and its cord was cut, it was covered and taken away by the midwife. She pleaded with them to let her see it just once. But the nurses and the midwife had their orders and they followed them to the letter.

The nurses held her down on the bed while the midwife took the baby away. She never knew whether it was a boy or girl. She wasn't difficult to restrain, weakened and distressed as she was by the pain and effort of giving birth.

A few weeks after the baby was born, her father came to see her. He told her she had brought shame on the family. She was not contrite and refused to plead for forgiveness. All she wanted was to see her child.

He refused even to acknowledge its existence.

He might well have taken her back into the family if it hadn't been for this final show of defiance. He told her she must atone for her sin. She must remain in the house and see no one. She could go out once a day at five o'clock in the afternoon but only into the garden and she must carry a bell to warn the world that she, who was not fit to be seen, was coming. He would get her a bell. God, he would get her a bell.

Those were the last words he ever spoke to her.

At first, she refused. She remained inside the house for several months. But then something changed in her. She seemed to accept the hopelessness of her situation and one day, at five in the afternoon, just as her father had said, she opened the door into the garden and stepped out, ringing the bell as she went. In the house, people came to the windows: servants, her mother, James, the cook. But not her father. He sat there, in his study, taking some perverse satisfaction in the rightness of his course of action. Everything was as it should be. The natural order of things had been restored.

After that, she came out every day, at the same time, always ringing the bell, just as her father had instructed her to do. It became something that people accepted, without even thinking, without finding it in any way unusual – just another feature of the harsh, unforgiving landscape in which they lived their lives.

Old Renwick was still a powerful man in the

community and few people, even the local minister or the one local policeman, would risk crossing him. And there was also another consideration, perhaps even more fundamental than that.

Most of the villagers felt that Renwick was in the right. His daughter had lain with a man out of marriage. No decent man would now marry her. She would be a burden on the family till the end of her days. In the eyes of the simple, no-shades-of-grey religion these people believed in, she had sinned. She had gone against God. And no man nor woman could do that with impunity.

Nancy's mother – who was in complete agreement with her husband – died a few years after the baby was born. Her father lived for another fourteen years. He was taken suddenly, of a stroke, riding back from market on a warm August night. James was driving the wagon. He heard a groan from his father. Turned and the old man slipped off the side of the wagon, dead before he hit the ground. Too easy a death, people said, for such a man.

James could have freed his sister and put an end to the appalling life which she had endured since the child was born. But he chose to keep things as they were. His father had made it clear this is what should happen and he couldn't go against his father, not even in death.

It could be that the damage was already done and that Renwick knew that his sister could no longer live in the world as a normal person. But he made no effort to find out. And it probably would have made no difference to him anyway.

After the death of the old man, the family became less central in the lives of the villagers. James completely lacked the power that his father had exercised over them. He neither sought it nor seemed to have any taste for it. It's arguable that someone in the village could have done something about Nancy Renwick. But, again, the feeling was that by this time the damage was done.

A young teacher, named Boyd, who came to the village school for a time, wrote to the Church authorities. And took the matter up with the Health Authority in Glasgow. But nothing was done and Boyd was moved on to another job somewhere out of the area. After that, Nancy was more or less forgotten by folk and they just got on with their lives which, God knows, were hard enough anyway.

When Mrs Weir finished this story, Grace nodded thoughtfully but said nothing. Mrs Weir had an uncanny feeling that nothing she had said had surprised the girl. It was almost as if the girl already knew the story. She even mentioned this to Simmie that night. He wasn't particularly interested. She agreed, on reflection, that it was probably just her imagination.

For some time, Mrs Weir had been suffering with the veins in her legs. These had become worse since Grace had arrived. In fact, as Mrs Weir had said to Simmie, it was just as well Grace had turned up because Mrs Weir doubted if she could have coped by herself.

Grace simply and quietly took over as and where she was needed. At first, for instance, Mrs Weir continued to take meals to both James and Nancy but this was just one of the many jobs Grace had soon taken off Mrs Weir's shoulders.

She would, just as Mrs Weir had done for so many years, take Nancy's tray into the hall, draw back the heavy velvet curtains and open the double doors that lay behind them. These doors were kept locked. Mrs Weir had given her the key for these when she started taking through Nancy's food. There was a second set of doors about five feet beyond the first. These were locked from the inside and only Nancy had a key. (She, too, was the only one who had keys for the blacked-out French windows at the back of the house which she used every day when she went out into the garden.) Grace would put the tray on the floor and take away the previous tray. Then she'd go back out, lock the doors and draw the curtains again. Nancy Renwick would, when she was ready, unlock the inner doors and take in the food.

Grace never complained about the extra work. She took it all on with good will and a kind of innocent, open eagerness that made Simmie less wary of her.

On the Thursday of the third or fourth week,

Simmie took her into Lochwinnoch. Usually, Simmie and Mrs Weir did this every month or so. She would shop and Simmie would visit the cattle market and have a few drinks with some of the men. This day, Mrs Weir's legs were worse than usual so she asked Grace if she'd like to go with Simmie. Grace was happy to comply but then she always complied, easily and willingly, with whatever Mrs Weir asked her to do. Simmie drove her to the back of the main church in Lochwinnoch where he usually parked and told her he'd meet her there in an hour and a half's time. She went off to work her way through the list Mrs Weir had given her. Simmie took a stroll round the market. It was mostly cattle with a few sheep in the stalls at the far end. He stopped to speak to the farmers and the buyers (mostly butchers) whom he'd come to know over the years. He looked in at the auction ring for a time. Then he made his way, as usual, to the Long Bar.

There were a group of men from the village in the bar. One of them was young Hugh Ferguson. Simmie nodded to a few of the men but went over to join Andrew Grey who had a farm up by Kilmacolm and his brother, Duncan, who ran the grocer's shop in Bridge of Weir. Hugh Ferguson was pleased to see Simmie come in. He knew Simmie had probably avoided him. But that didn't matter. He'd have a word with him anyway.

A Child of Air

Young Ferguson had been curious about the girl from the moment he'd heard about her. Ferguson was a farmer, in his late twenties. He had inherited one of the few good farms near Millarston when his father died and had run it passably since. He hadn't married though most people knew he was seeing a widow in Lochwinnoch, a woman in her forties, who hoped Ferguson would marry her. He, of course, had no intention of doing so. Simmie didn't like Ferguson. He was sly, callous and often drunk and Simmie had listened to him brag in bars about what he did to his widow and what he could make her do to him. But in a community like that you had to try and stay on good terms with your neighbours: you never knew when you might need their help.

After twenty minutes or so, Ferguson came over. He asked how things were going with the girl. There was some talk among the four men about what had happened to Clair and how close she'd come to dying. Simmie didn't say much, always wary of Ferguson, but he did mention that he'd brought the girl into town with him. Ferguson boasted to Andrew Grey about the price he'd got for a bull that morning and then went back over to the bar to refill his glass. Simmie didn't pay him any more attention. When he looked round, ten or fifteen minutes later, and couldn't see Ferguson, he thought no more about it.

Simmie stayed in the bar longer than he'd

planned. He wasn't in any way drunk when he came out: he'd had a few whiskies, just enough to feel good about the world. He made his way down the alley at the side of the church. After the market-day bustle, the small country town with its straight grey streets intersecting each other was beginning to return to its lifeless self. The air was cool and slightly damp. It would probably rain before long.

As he approached the back of the church, he heard some laughing and voices. Slightly raucous, teasing, grating. There were still several cars parked there. These blocked his view at first.

He knew something was wrong right away. He seemed, almost instantly, to know what it was even before he saw anything. He hurried, slipping sideways between the cars, to where he could see that Ferguson had Grace pinned against the black Austin. He was holding her there with one hand. In the other, he held her basket of groceries. He offered this to her and then snatched it away again just as she went to touch it.

'Come on, gie us a kiss. Then ye can have yir basket back.'

'Let me go.'

'A kiss. That's a'.'

'Please.'

'I can wait. I've a' night tae wait. I'm sure it'd be worth it.'

Two of Ferguson's cronies were looking on,

sniggering. He heard Simmie before he saw him. He was turning towards Simmie when Simmie pulled him away from the girl with one hand and hit him in the face with the other. The blow sent Ferguson sprawling across the cobblestones. The basket and its contents fell around him. The cronies backed away smartly.

Simmie regretted hitting him immediately. But it was done now. And it was up to Ferguson what followed. Simmie wasn't afraid of the younger man. He waited, ready for him.

Ferguson grinned up at Simmie from the ground, wiping away the trickle of blood from under his nose.

'What's wrong, Simmie? Jist tryin tae be friendly, welcome the lassie properly. That's a'.'

'Get.'

'What – ye want tae get in there yirsel, Simmie? Cannae say I blame ye.'

Simmie moved towards him. Ferguson held up a hand, to indicate he wasn't going to push it any further. The girl was picking up the shopping and putting it back into the basket. Simmie kept his eyes on Ferguson. The cronies smiled nervously, not sure whether this was going to turn into something or not. Ferguson stood up slowly, grinning, as if this was all just a joke.

'Nae offence.'

Simmie said nothing. Ferguson moved off with the other two men. Before they had gone a few steps Simmie could hear them laughing at something Ferguson had said.

'I'm sorry, Grace. Too much drink. That's a' that's wrong wi them.'

Grace was quiet but didn't seem too upset. Simmie helped her pick up the last of the shopping.

'I shoulda been back sooner.'

'I'm a' right, Mr Weir.'

'Are ye sure?'

She smiled.

'I'll niver hear the end i this fae Mrs Weir.'

'Let's no say anythin to Mrs Weir. It wid jist upset her.'

Simmie was surprised.

'Aye, okay. If ye say so.'

'I'm fine, Mr Weir. Really.'

The girl set his mind at ease with a quite definite nod and got into the car. Simmie joined her, relieved – if a little uneasily – at this unexpected reprieve.

It was generally fairly dark inside the two rooms where Nancy Renwick lived. They were large rooms. One had been the main reception room when the house had been full and noisy with life. It was long and high with a bay window at the front but the heavy velvet curtains were kept closed, blocking the light and the world outside equally effectively.

She slept in this room. Her bed was pushed against the wall, near the curtains. The room was dusty and there was a pervasive smell of dampness. She tended to spend most of her time in the other room. It was smaller and easier to keep warm in the winter. The dining table with its fourteen chairs was still there but pushed back against the wall. She had one chair at the table on the side nearest the fire. This was where she ate. This had been her chair all her life, from as early as she could remember. She had sat at it as a child, rubbing her fingers back and forwards over the infinitely smooth, warm ball of wood at the top of the right hand leg. There was another one of these at the left. It was exactly the same but she had never found the same degree of comfort there.

Her meals were given to her at fixed, regular times; breakfast at eight, lunch at twelve-thirty, dinner at six-thirty, supper at ten. She'd hear the outer doors being opened and the tray being slid in and then the doors being closed again. She'd get up and take the tray, set the cutlery and the dishes on the table and sit down to eat. Mrs Weir knew that Nancy had been ill several times. Sometimes she hadn't gone outside and at other times her food hadn't been touched. On one occasion she had sent a note asking for morphine for a toothache. James had allowed her two bottles. After this, presumably, the nerve in the tooth had died or the trouble had remedied itself in some other way.

Nancy sometimes read or did intricate, difficult needlepoint. Mostly, though, she listened to the radio. She didn't know where this had come from. One day, five or maybe six years ago, she'd gone into the garden as usual and when she came back the radio was there: a large smooth mahogany box with fine, dark green netting across the front. This was the only time when James showed some consideration for his sister or gave any indication that he was aware of the isolation in which she lived out her days.

Nancy had no idea what the radio was. She did nothing with it at first. She'd touch it, run her fingers over it. She would put her hands on the large black bakelite knobs with serrated edges. She felt that they would go, that they would turn. But she was afraid of the thing, unsure of its purpose in her life.

It was many days before she finally turned one of the dials far enough for it to click on and splutter into life. Nothing happened at first, then there was a series of little cracks and pops and a voice came into the room that had been silent for so long. She had turned it off again almost immediately, frightened. She had no conception of what this thing was. She related it to what she knew or had heard of – which was the telephone. She thought at first that it was someone talking directly and only to her, but she didn't recognize the voice. It wasn't James and it wasn't her father. (She wasn't absolutely sure but she thought her father was dead. She had, a long time ago, seen a funeral leave the house and had felt it was his, though no one had communicated this to her in any way.) She knew that with a telephone you could talk back to the person on the other end of the line. She could see no way of doing that with this thing.

She tried talking to it with the radio switched off. Nothing happened.

She turned it on again and listened. The voice came through. It wasn't speaking to her, she was sure of that. It had an English accent and it was talking about a railway accident in Salford. She tried talking back tentatively. But the voice didn't stop for her and continued over everything she said. Then it changed to something about a man who had murdered his wife. Then it was about a football match in Newcastle. She left it on, watching it as much as listening to it.

She liked the sound of other voices in the room. Sometimes it played music, not like any music she had ever heard before but even the music was better than silence. It filled the void.

She was disappointed when, late at night, the national anthem was played and the voices and the music stopped again. She could hear a low noise, like someone rustling tissue paper on the other side of the room but that was all. Every so often this would be punctuated by a fierce bout of crackling. She didn't turn it off that night and was surprised to hear a voice in the rooms when she woke in the morning. It was a man's voice, talking about an outbreak of Malta Fever among cattle in

Wales. It didn't matter really what he was saying, just that someone was saying something. She left it on and gradually the radio became part of the fabric of her quiet, wasted life.

It's impossible to be precise about when Grace started going into Nancy's rooms.

Nancy said it began several weeks after the girl arrived. Although she was cut off from the house, Nancy had some sense of what happened in it. She had heard the girl talking to Mrs Weir and had seen her taking out washing to the side garden.

She had no idea how Grace got into her rooms. She was asked about this many times but never came up with any very satisfactory explanation. Nancy told the psychiatrists who interviewed her later that Grace would suddenly be there and then just as suddenly disappear. But Nancy Renwick was not generally regarded as the most reliable of witnesses. Those years of isolation and virtual imprisonment had taken their toll on her sanity, though several of the doctors who examined her mentioned her lucidity and apparently acute memory: one at least added a dissenting appendix to the report on her and stated that, in his opinion, she was perfectly sane and remarkably untouched by the strangeness of her life for the last twenty or so years.

According to Nancy, she was sitting by the fire, listening to the radio, when she heard a noise. She

looked round. The girl was standing in the doorway between the two rooms. She held one hand
out to her, in a gesture that conveyed there was no
need to worry and that she meant no harm. She
smiled slightly but was clearly concerned at the
effect of her presence on Nancy.

'There's nae need tae be afraid.'

Nancy looked at the girl for a long moment. For
some reason, right from the beginning, she felt
that she could trust her. Something told her she
had nothing to fear.

'Who are ye?'

'Ye know who I am.' There was a slight pause
before the girl added, 'Ye've seen me outside.'

Grace helped Nancy back into her chair. She
held her hand. Someone else touching her. The
feeling was odd – pleasant and comforting, very
comforting. That was what she remembered vividly and mentioned most frequently to the psychiatrists whenever she was asked about this first
meeting.

Grace walked about the room, looking closely at
everything.

'What are ye doin in here?' It was an effort for
her to find the words. It was strange to hear her
own voice, which sounded somehow too loud for
the room.

'I came in tae see ye.'

'But no one's allowed in here.'

'I know.'

'I'll be punished.'

81

'Naeb'dy's goin tae punish ye for this. Naeb'dy will find out.'

Nancy believed the girl. There was something in her voice that smoothed away any doubts or worries.

Nancy wasn't sure how long the girl stayed that first time. She asked Nancy questions about herself, how she had managed in here. She looked at the radio. She kept saying there was nothing to worry about and that she would go if Nancy wanted.

After a time – and without Nancy being aware of it – the girl was simply not there again. Nancy went into the next room to see if she was there. She wasn't. Nancy tried the doors. They were locked.

Five

～

About a month after the girl's arrival, Mrs
Weir began to spend some time in the
village. Mrs Weir was on the unofficial
committee of women who organized the harvest
dance. They'd get together several afternoons a
week in the church hall where the dance was held.
They spent hours deciding who was going to
provide what food, who was going to make the
tea, who was going to bake the cakes and the
scones, who was going to make the harvest bread.
This hardly changed from year to year but it was
always discussed at length before any work was
begun. Once all of that was settled, the women
would make and hang up decorations. And carry
out – or commandeer the men to carry out – any
repairs that were needed around the hall. This
was generally quite a good time in the village: the
main work of the year had been done. There was

the opportunity to relax, rest, prepare for the winter. This process of easing back from exertion, passing from one season to another, getting ready for the stillness of winter was all part of the natural rhythm of life in the village.

The church hall was a red-painted, corrugated shed behind the church. It stood on the main road out of the village, the last building you passed if you were going up towards Renwick House. The inner walls had been panelled with wood which made it seem somehow more substantial from inside than it appeared from the outside. There was a stage, or raised platform, at one end. A large black pot-bellied stove squatted in a corner, inside a wire cage (to stop the children from burning themselves), and made the hall warm on even the coldest and stormiest of days. There were windows, narrow and long, almost church-like, with frosted glass and red curtains, along both sides of the hall so, during the day at least, the hall felt light and airy and somehow even bigger than it really was. The women of the village kept it clean and in good order. The men were marshalled into helping out with major jobs such as painting and keeping the roof sound as and when necessary. The hall was well used for Sunday schools, bible classes, women's meetings and the occasional political or farmers' meeting. It was the one place in the community where everyone, or pretty much everyone, would come together at some point.

Mrs Weir took Grace with her on these trips. Simmie would run them into the village in the car in the early afternoon and come back for them around five. The mood in the hall on these afternoons was light, happy, easy.

The women would talk to each other almost constantly as they worked. There was a kind of excitement, or exhilaration, in the air. There were jokes, stories about neighbours and recipes and tips were exchanged. The mood tended to heighten and increase the closer they approached the dance itself. This was the first time most of the village women had seen Grace or spoken to her.

They were a little cautious, or even suspicious, of her at first but this didn't last for long. Grace may have been from outside the village but they soon accepted her pretty much as one of them. She would say very little during these sessions. She'd smile shyly at their jokes or look down, as if embarrassed, when they teased her about having to find her a man and how maybe they'd do that at the dance. Afterwards, the women – like everyone else – realized how little she had told them about herself. They knew she was an orphan. They knew she had been at Quarrier's Homes but some thought she had worked there for a time while others said she'd been brought up there from a baby. One point they were all clear on was that they were fond of her. It was more than that, though – she seemed somehow vulnerable and they felt, certainly the older ones did, some protective urge towards her, as if she were a child who needed to be looked after, as if she weren't quite sturdy enough to cope with the hardness and unpleasantness of this world. She had always seemed so small and slight to them, as if, as one of them said, 'Wan gust of wind wid lift her away'. Another factor that predisposed them towards her was that she became quite interested in them and their lives: she would ask questions about relatives or parents who had long since died and moved away and she would listen attentively to the answers. This wasn't something that the women minded: few people object to talking about their own families and are quite pleased to come across someone who seems equally interested.

There was only one incident of any note concerning the girl that took place during this period. It's difficult, as with all of this story, to be sure of the truth. No one could say with any certainty whether this really did happen or if it was simply a product of the mythmaking that rose up around the girl after she'd gone. It was an incident that Maisie Innes witnessed at the village hall one day. (Walter Innes owned the bar and the shop in the village, Maisie was his wife: Walter died during the war, Maisie ran both the bar and the shop by herself until the late fifties.) It was as if this was her own little part of the story, like a piece of private property and she guarded it jealously. It's a tiny little incident and possibly unimportant but it would probably be wrong to pass over it.

Grace was sitting with Maisie and old Mrs Campbell, a widow, in the hall one afternoon. Mrs Campbell had brought in a small statue which her husband had brought back from China. He had been in the navy for the best part of ten years and had travelled all over the world before he came back to the village, found himself a wife in Mrs Campbell, who was herself originally from Houston, and settled down to work twenty acres that he leased from Old John Renwick. The statue was a curious thing and there were probably quite a few dotted here and there about the world, though no two of them would ever have been quite the same.

It was of a sailor, in a British uniform. Presumably, similar figures existed of sailors in French or American or Dutch uniforms. All of these were fired up in the pottery and the uniforms hand-painted on to the white porcelain. But the faces were left blank. The idea was that the sailor would buy one and his face would be painted on to this tiny blank piece of porcelain. Even the hair would be painted in. This was the only picture, as it were, that Mrs Campbell had of her husband. It had been painted over sixty years ago, when he would have been barely twenty. But she swore it was a good likeness. She had brought it in to show Grace, having talked about it a few days before. Maisie Innes looked at it closely. She'd heard about it before and she'd known George

Campbell. She laughed when she saw it, surprised at how much it resembled the man she'd known. It was uncanny.

The face was barely an inch and a half high and yet it looked like George Campbell to the life. The girl looked at it, too. She seemed very taken with it. One or two other women, some of whom had seen it before, came over. It was one of these women who, as she was handing it back to Mrs Campbell, let it slip. It struck Mrs Campbell's knee and slipped off towards the floor. Mrs Campbell grabbed at it and missed it and closed her eyes as it struck the floor. She therefore didn't really see what happened but Maisie Innes was to one side and she maintained that she could see the statue clearly strike the hard wooden floor and break into several pieces. Or at least she was sure that was what she had seen but then it was exactly at that moment that Grace bent down. Her hand went to the statue, blocking Maisie's view. Mrs Campbell was crying, afraid to open her eyes. Grace said, 'It's a'right.'

Mrs Campbell shivered.

'It's broken. I know it.'

'No, no. It's a'right.'

Grace straightened up and held the statue up. It was in one piece. Maisie Innes said, 'I saw it. It was broken.'

Grace shook her head.

'Well, it's no broken now.'

She held the statue to the light and turned it

round and round. It was in one piece. There were
no fractures. It was exactly as it had been when
Mrs Campbell dropped it. The old woman took it
greedily into her own hands, barely able to
believe her good fortune. Maisie Innes looked at
Grace, who seemed only concerned to reassure
the older woman.

'No, it's no broken, is it?'

'Lucky, eh?'

There was a last general burst of activity on the
land and around the house those few weeks
before the winter set in properly. Simmie did
what he could in the way of digging before the
earth became too heavy with water and too difficult to work. He did some pruning, cut the grass
one last time, began to bring those plants that
could be moved back into the warmth and security of the greenhouse. There was no great edge of
desperation in any of this but it was a kind of
undeclared race against time, to get as much done
as possible before the first frost came and winter
set in with a vengeance.

It was much the same with James Renwick. He
now worked only three fields of the many acres
that still belonged to the house. Two of these
fields had been planted with barley which had
been harvested and sold at the end of September
for a reasonable price. These fields had now to be
cleared, razed and turned over with the plough.
He did all of this himself, even the ploughing,

guiding and manhandling the plough behind two great Clydesdale horses that he hired from another farmer by the day. The third field was given over to sugar beet. This was still in the ground in the middle of November but it had to be lifted quickly now or else the water would rot it. He took on just one man from the village and together the two of them started to lift the beets. It was unrelenting heart-breaking, back-breaking work – bending over, lifting, moving on. Most days it was raining and the long, silvery beets would stick in the ground and the leaves come away in your hand. Renwick worked all the hours of daylight. He'd come home to eat and sleep and then go back out again the next morning. Sometimes, he was so exhausted he didn't bother to wash or change his clothes.

This went on for ten days with just one Sunday off when he rose at five and drove to Hawick where he had agreed to preach that afternoon. The man from the village gave up after four days, saying he wasn't going to work like an animal for two shillings a day and who would blame him? Certainly no one in the village.

On the eleventh day, two lorries Renwick had hired came up to the field. Renwick loaded the beets himself and went with them to the market in Paisley. The price was less than he'd hoped for but, like all farmers, he had to take what he could get. He couldn't afford to take two lorryloads of beet back home and bring them another day when the price might have risen – but then the buyers knew that, didn't they?

It was around this time that Renwick noticed a change in the girl. It was quite subtle at first. When she brought him his meals, for instance, she no longer kept her eyes down. She would look at him directly, full in the eye, so much so that he found it, at times, disconcerting. She no longer seemed afraid of him.

Once, towards the end of November, she brushed up against him as she was laying his meal on the table. It was just the briefest of moments during which the softness of her breast moulded itself against the bone in his shoulder. The shock of it surged through his body, bringing a wonderful but transient sense of physical release. She didn't look at him. She seemed totally unaware of the tiny, intimate accident.

One day, Ferguson came out to the house to take back some tools and a harness that he'd lent Simmie. Simmie had heard from Mrs Weir that Ferguson had been hanging around the village hall, trying to have a word with Grace, but that the girl had avoided him. She didn't need Simmie to tell her that they would do better to keep Ferguson away from the girl: Mrs Weir knew his reputation as well as anyone.

The tools in question had been lying around for months and Simmie was fairly certain they were only an excuse for Ferguson to come round and maybe catch a glimpse of Grace. Ferguson said nothing about the incident in Lochwinnoch. It was as if it had never happened. His manner was friendly, perhaps over-friendly. Simmie was cautious with him: he didn't want to pretend Lochwinnoch hadn't happened but he would be glad if it could be forgotten. You needed your neighbours too much in a place like that. You tried, as best you could, to get on with people.

Ferguson's eyes kept moving around, looking to the house, but Grace stayed inside that day. Ferguson asked about her but Simmie said very little, just that she had settled in fine. Ferguson reminded him that the dance was coming up and he hoped she'd be there. Simmie didn't know if they'd be going this year, what with Mrs Weir's legs. Ferguson said he'd be delighted to take care of the girl. Simmie gave him a look – realizing now that the incident in Lochwinnoch would not be so easily forgotten after all – and told him he had to get on with his work. Ferguson grinned, leaving Simmie in no doubt as to just how he meant to take care of the girl. Simmie knew it was a provocation but it wasn't one he would rise to here or now.

Ferguson loaded the tools and harness into the back of his van and drove off.

According to Nancy, Grace came to see her again a few nights after that first visit.

This would have been at the end of October or

possibly the first week in November. She didn't
know how the girl got into her rooms. It happened exactly as before: she heard a noise from
the other room, went through and the girl was
standing there, just inside the double doors. She
said, 'I'll go if ye like. I won't stay unless ye want
me to.'

Nancy shook her head – no, she didn't want the
girl to go.

That second visit was fairly short. Grace sat
with her near the fire. She touched Nancy's hand
briefly. Nancy couldn't think what to say or even
what to make of Grace. She just sat there and
watched the girl – puzzled, confused, grateful that
she had returned.

The radio was playing as usual – a concert of
dance music from The Savoy. The girl began to
speak. She told Nancy what had been happening
in the house: just the small domestic details of
everyday life. She talked about Mrs Weir and
Simmie, and how Mrs Weir's leg had been bothering her more recently. She didn't mention
James – at least, that was Nancy's recollection. She
left after perhaps ten or fifteen minutes and
Nancy was sorry to see her go. She wanted to ask
her to stay but didn't dare. Grace opened the
inside set of double doors quite easily. Nancy had
believed she was the only one with keys to these
but the girl must somehow have obtained a set:
that seemed the most likely explanation for the
ease with which she was able to come and go.

During November, Grace came to visit Nancy more often until she was coming almost every night. Nancy looked forward to her visits. She felt comfortable with her. She was glad to be a part of the outside world again, and to hear some of the things that were happening there. When Grace started to go with Mrs Weir to the village hall, she was able to bring Nancy news of the people in the village. Nancy didn't know many of the younger villagers but she often knew the family names or the parents of some of the people Grace mentioned. There were still many of the older villagers whom she remembered particularly well, though they hadn't been old when she'd first known them. Some people, of course, had moved away or died. The girl was always, it seemed to Nancy, cautious about telling her when this had happened to someone she'd asked about. She could see that it upset Nancy. It brought her hard up against the fact that time had moved on, despite the few signs of it having done so in her own tiny world. They would listen to the radio and Nancy would chat about the news she had heard that day in the village hall so that soon the village became repopulated for Nancy, with a cast of characters whom she knew and could see in her mind's eye even though she had never laid eyes on them. She knew whose husband was drinking too much, whose farm was all but owned by the bank now, whose cattle had come down with a virus and been destroyed, who had done well in the lamb

sales, who had a child that had gone off to
university in Glasgow on a scholarship, who had
decided to emigrate to Canada. In passing on all
these tiny inconsequential details, it was almost
as if Grace was making her a part of the world
again, drawing her back into a life from which she
had been so comprehensively excluded.

As they became more comfortable with each
other, Grace talked more about herself. But all she
ever gave were glimpses – of her time at Quarrier's Homes in Bridge of Weir, of a few months
spent in a large hotel in Glasgow, or a summer
season at the Royal Hotel in Ayr.

One night, Grace asked Nancy to step into the
hall with her, just to see what it was like outside
the rooms. Nancy refused point blank. It took
Grace some time to calm her down again. For the
first time, Nancy began to feel frightened of her.

'I want ye tae leave here wi me.'

'No, I cannae do that.'

'Ye could.'

'James wouldnae allow it.'

'He couldnae stop ye.'

'He would.'

'No.'

'I don't want tae leave.'

She was becoming agitated and upset.

'It's a'right,' said the girl, 'we don't need tae
think about this now. Plenty of time. Plenty of
time.'

★ ★ ★

Renwick was determined not to become involved with the girl.

He had been tempted often enough by other women who had worked in the house but he knew it was dangerous. It made him vulnerable. Clair MacIndoe had been such a risk. He still didn't understand why she had never caused problems for him. He had been lucky. He knew that. He also knew that he was unlikely to be so lucky twice.

Renwick was baffled by the power of these forces that he contained within himself. He didn't understand their nature. They went directly against everything that he had been brought up to think and feel about the world. Those forces were never recognized in the world to which his parents had introduced him. Or rather, if they ever were recognized, it was only in terms of the most utter disapproval. They had no place in his life as it ought to be lived.

Given all this, it was almost a relief to Renwick when the accident happened to Clair MacIndoe. They'd heard that she'd been kept in the hospital and that part of her arm had been amputated when gangrene set in. Renwick had been sorry for her and sent her some money but he was glad that she wouldn't – in all likelihood – be coming back to the house.

He could start again. He wouldn't let that situation – or anything like it – ever arise again. And yet, he found his thoughts being drawn more and more towards the girl. He could be working in the fields for hours, tidying up after the harvesting and breaking the ground for the winter. His clothes would be soaked through and clinging to his skin. His back and thighs would be aching, beyond belief, from the bending and digging, bending and digging. His fingers would be caked with clay and the skin torn open by stones and roots buried in the ground. And still he would find himself thinking of her. Thinking, more precisely, of her body.

It was as if his own body and mind were two quite separate entities, each capable of its own independent life. These lives, of the mind and body, were totally divorced from each other and often even at odds with each other. They co-existed with each other but it was an uneasy and potentially destructive accommodation. Renwick would try to lose himself in his work but his mind kept finding its way back to the girl. It was like the mountain burns he used to dam up as a child with boulders and branches and clods of grass ripped from the ground: unless you provided a way for some of the water to run off, the pressure would build to the point where it simply swept the dam aside, no matter how strong you tried to make it.

Six

The psychiatrists who interviewed Nancy later were fascinated, in a clinical sense, by how her experiences had affected her.

On the one hand, she had a good grasp of what was happening in the world outside (due presumably to the radio). She had been unusually careful of her appearance, they felt. They were surprised at how well she had continued to groom herself throughout her twenty years or more of confinement. She cut and washed her own hair. She bathed regularly in the little bathroom which adjoined the back room: previously, the entrance to this had been from the hall but, immediately after the birth of her child, her father had had that door blocked off and the wall knocked through in readiness for her, so that no one but she could use that room. She looked after her clothes, mended them when they needed it and made new ones when the old could no longer be repaired. Whenever she needed anything such as material or thread, she'd put a note on her tray.

A few of those notes were retained by the psychiatrists: there is nothing on them other than a list of requirements. No words about herself, no indication who wrote the notes or to whom they were addressed – in other words, they were totally devoid of any human or personal touch whatsoever.

The psychiatrists also noted that Nancy had obvious difficulty in speaking. She would frequently stop in mid-sentence, searching for a word or phrase which more often than not would not come and then she'd simply trail off into silence.

They were not surprised, given all of this, and the girl's sudden appearance in her life, that Nancy soon became convinced that Grace was her long lost child.

Nancy remembered very clearly the night when the idea first came to her. Grace had washed her hair. They were drying it by the fire. Nancy sat with her head bent over and hair hanging down in front of the fire. Grace brushed it out again and again. If Nancy moved too close to the fire, Grace would gently ease her back, saying it wouldn't do her hair any good. All the time, tirelessly, she kept brushing Nancy's hair. It was the gentleness of all this that made Nancy suddenly articulate, but only in her own mind, the thought that had been there for some time. The girl had come here for a purpose. She had come to the house expressly to see Nancy. And she was the right age.

It was true that Nancy had never known what sex her child was. But, set against everything else, that seemed a minor area of doubt. She had no idea how the girl had found out about her or why she had come back to her. She didn't even, at that time, say anything to the girl. She was frightened by the idea, but also irresistibly drawn to it. She was terrified that it might be true, and equally terrified that it might not. She said nothing to the girl. She allowed her to go on brushing her hair and lifting it up towards the coals, like one of the servants, long forgotten, used to do when she was very young.

One evening, Grace and Mrs Weir stayed later than usual at the village hall.

They were putting up some of the decorations for the dance and Mrs Weir had told Renwick they'd be late, not that he'd paid any great attention to her. Simmie would get the Master some food and then come down for the women around seven.

It had turned dark soon after five that day. There was rain in the air but it hadn't started yet. You could smell a freshness on the wind and the clouds, lit intermittently by the moon, raced across the moors, great grey tumbling shapes. At about quarter past seven, Grace came outside to see if there was any sign of Simmie with the car.

The wind was rushing through the trees behind the village hall. Leaves that had lain in silent heaps along the side of the road went slithering and rolling across the road now, adding their own particular noise to the night. She looked up the road towards the house. There was no one on the road down from the big house. She turned and walked along the side of the hall, in the direction of the village. It probably occurred to her that Simmie may well have taken advantage of his wife's absence to stop off at Innes's Bar in the village. She walked to the far end of the hall, passing the windows that laid their widening rectangles of yellow light on the road.

Ferguson watched her coming towards him. He was quite sure she didn't know he was there. He had been there for some time. Ever since Mrs Weir had started bringing the girl to the hall, Ferguson had made it a habit to pass that way when he could in the hope that he might get a word with her. He was sure that if he could just get her to talk to him he would have her. That was all you needed: to get talking to them. Once you had that little piece of trust, you could build on it. Soon you'd have them in bed, doing whatever you wanted. That, at any rate, had been Ferguson's experience with the women he'd known.

'Hello, lass.' She jumped, clearly frightened. Ferguson moved towards her but didn't touch her.

'What are ye doin here?'

'Just passin.'

'I've got to go back in.'

'No. No yet.' He grabbed her arm.

'Mrs Weir's in there.'

'She'll be fine. Come you here.' He pulled her towards him, pressed his body against hers. 'Why ye bein so unfriendly?'

'Let me go.'

'Ye don't really want me tae let ye go. Ye want it. Don't ye?'

He pressed his groin against her belly.

'I don't want anythin!' she screamed at him, with such force that it made him laugh.

Ferguson bent down to kiss her. She struggled and kicked at him. He laughed again and wrapped both strong arms round her, beginning to draw up her skirt. She wriggled and writhed in his arms, utterly powerless to break away from him.

It was then that car headlights swept across the trees on the other side of the road. Ferguson released her and backed away.

'See ye at the dance, eh?'

He watched her as she walked back to the front door and waited for Simmie to pull up. Part of the reason why he waited was that he thought she would tell Simmie and Simmie might well come after him. But she didn't say anything very much to Simmie. They went into the hall together and came out, having switched off all the lights, with

107

Mrs Weir. Then they drove off.

Ferguson relaxed and grinned. He took this as a good sign. She wanted it. Of course she did. She just needed some encouragement.

The touching began to happen more often. Her arm would brush against his. The wonderful rounded firmness of her hips would press against him as she cleared away his dishes. She would look at him, too, full in the eyes and with a hint of a smile as if she knew exactly what these moments meant to him and what effect they had on him. When he was being questioned by the police, Renwick said that sometimes he felt she could see right into his heart and read all the dark secrets contained there.

She would – incredibly – tease him sometimes. She would chide him if he left food on his plate, as if she were talking to a mischievous child. She told him that he should eat what she'd brought 'right now' because it would get cold quick if he left it, which he sometimes did.

Once, when she brought him a boiled egg, there was no salt on the tray. He said it didn't matter. She said, No, she would fetch the salt. And she did. She went all the way downstairs and came back a few brief moments later with the salt cellar. She placed it on the desk. He said, Thank you. She nodded and said, 'An egg wi'out salt is like a kiss wi'out a moustache.'

She was looking right at him again. Staring

straight into his eyes, with that half-smile playing on her lips. And then she turned and was gone again.

He began to watch her even more closely when she came into the study with his meals. His eyes would follow the shadow of her shift underneath the crisp white cotton blouse she wore. He would trace out the hidden curves of her body under her dark serge skirt, which rustled against her petticoats as she moved around the room. He could smell the sweat, never strong, lingering on her skin. Sometimes, she had just washed and all he could detect was the delicately pungent aroma of soap.

He started going up to her room when she and Mrs Weir were out at the village hall. He crept quietly – although there was no one to hear him – along that damp bare-boarded corridor where he and Nancy had played as children. He went into the room and looked around. There were few personal items. She hadn't attempted in any way to make the room her own. The battered brown case now stood empty beside the walnut-faced wardrobe. Her clothes hung in the wardrobe or were folded neatly in the drawers by the window. He moved his hands in among the clean cotton underwear. He made sure he disturbed nothing and that, if he did, he left it all exactly as he found it. Sometimes, he would tug the bedcovers back and slip his hand between the sheets – just cold and smooth – but again he would make sure he left this exactly as it had been.

When he was up there, he would sometimes think he heard someone coming along the corridor, even though he knew there was no one else in the house except Nancy. He would hurry out and look up and down the corridor, breathless, waiting for retribution which never came.

Once he went up there at night, when she was sleeping. The door was closed but not locked. He turned the handle slowly. It made no noise. He leaned against the door, hardly pushing, and it opened a few inches. She didn't stir. He could barely see her. Just her hair and an arm thrown across the covers. As his eyes became accustomed to the darkness, he could make out the outline of her body underneath the covers. One knee was slightly raised. But he could, in truth, see very little. After a few moments, she moved, turning her arm first to one side and then the other before she settled. He'd caught a glimpse of her face, eyes closed, mouth open, as she said something in her sleep, something which he didn't catch. He pulled the door shut, heart thumping, listening in case he'd wakened her. But it was all quite silent. She was still clearly asleep.

He hurried back down the corridor, still afraid that someone – he didn't know who – would find him out. Even as he did so, he felt sure he would be back. It was as if it were written in a book.

★ ★ ★

Nancy began looking forward to Grace's visits more and more.

Grace generally came about ten o'clock at night. And she was now coming every night, rather than every second or third night as she had done at first. If she was a few moments later than usual, Nancy would get agitated. And when Grace did eventually turn up, she'd be slightly cool with her, though this never lasted for very long. Nancy began asking Grace to stay longer with her. Grace was firm on this and was always gone by eleven-thirty or midnight at the latest.

At the beginning, Nancy had wondered exactly how Grace came into and out of her rooms. There was no mystery about that now. She had watched Grace come and go, using a key, many times. She asked Grace about this key but the girl was always vague about it, simply saying, when pressed, that she'd 'found it lyin around some-where'.

Nancy estimated, as best she could, that it would have been around the fourth or fifth of December. They were sitting in the back room, listening to the radio. Nancy had been showing Grace how to do stem stitch on a piece of white-work embroidery and Grace was now practising this on her own. Her whole attention was focused on the piece of cloth in its frame and the needle. Her mouth was slightly open and Nancy could see her tongue held just between her teeth in an almost child-like parody of concentration. She looked so vulnerable, so innocent that Nancy wanted to protect her from the world. Nancy was fully aware of the irony of this: the idea that she, who had lived out of the world for so long, could protect anyone was laughable.

Grace had been to the village hall that day and had already shared with Nancy her latest crop of gossip about life in the village. There had been nothing of great importance: Ellen Makin, whose mother Nancy had sometimes played with as a child, had just given birth to a boy; the postman, Alec McAuley, had been drunk the night before and was late with the post again; Innes, who owned the shop and the bar in the village, had refused credit to two more families who would now almost certainly have to leave the village and look for work in Glasgow or further afield.

Nancy had been listening to Al Bowlly singing on a live broadcast from a dancehall. She knew his voice, even when the announcer made no mention of the singer, as was common in those days. She loved that sweet, pure voice that seemed to belong to a better world – a world where everything was as it should be. He'd sung two songs – 'Melancholy Baby' and 'Got a Date with an Angel'. Then the band played on its own and Nancy lost interest in the radio after that, though it remained on as always. She was still watching Grace working on the embroidery. Grace finished part of a flower motif and held it up to Nancy for a verdict.

'It's good.'

'Ye think so?'

Nancy studied it more closely.

'Couldnae dae better myself.'

'Really?'

'Aye. Really.'

The girl smiled, clearly pleased with this show of approval.

Nancy watched her start on the next tiny part of the motif.

'D'ye mind if I ask ye somethin?'

'No.'

'What age are ye?'

The girl stopped. Nancy thought she looked almost reluctant to answer. Not because she wanted to lie. But because she knew exactly what question was being asked and how the answer would, irrevocably, change everything.

'Why d'ye ask?'

'Just curious.'

'I'm twenty-three.'

Nancy's child would also be twenty three.

'When's yir birthday?'

There was a kind of sadness in the girl's eyes. As the moment of silence went on and on, Nancy began to have her doubts again. Maybe the girl was just thrown by being asked this question so directly and so suddenly. Maybe she did understand what Nancy was really asking but didn't know the right answer. That could be quite possible.

'Third of March.'

'What year?'

'1911.'

Nancy sat back in her chair. She looked straight ahead. That was exactly when her own child had been born.

The girl was just watching her, waiting to see what she would do. Nancy began to weep. Suddenly, she opened her arms and took the girl to her. The girl, too, was weeping by this time. She stayed there, in Nancy's arms, allowing Nancy to hold her.

Seven

Renwick had a sense of things spinning out of control. Sometimes he felt as if he didn't want to stop whatever was happening from running its course, as he knew that it would. He welcomed it, even urged it on – though he couldn't have said with any clarity at that time exactly what he thought *was* happening.

There were times when he would suddenly find himself at his desk or on his bed with no sense of what he had been doing before that instant, or whether he had been there for a few moments or several hours. His mind was a blank at these times. He didn't know whether he had been sleeping or lost consciousness. When he found himself at his desk, he would look at what he had written and often it made no sense at all. Sometimes it was just one word or phrase repeated over and over again. Always, it was in the same copperplate handwriting which was undoubtedly his and yet which was also far neater, far more controlled, than his own normal script.

He claimed – later – to be in great discomfort and pain during this time. There were dizzy spells which transformed themselves into agonizing headaches, always spiking out from the same point at the base of his skull. At night, he slept very little and never peacefully. He woke often, shivering and sweating, still half-immersed in appalling dreams, most of which involved his father. These dreams nearly always ended with the sound of his father's footsteps as he came up the stairs and along the corridor to punish him.

Through all of this, Renwick was still tormented by thoughts of the girl. He could remember, with heart-breaking intensity, the softness and warmth of those moments where her body had touched his. Sometimes, when he was sitting at his desk or lying in bed, he could actually feel her hair against his cheek. It was as if she were there, laying her head against his.

It's hard to establish chronology from this part of Renwick's account with any precision. But it seems that it was roughly during the first week of December when he went back up to the girl's room, knowing that she would be there.

He had no idea what time it was. It was dark, that was all he could remember. His mind was a chaos of different thought streams: fear that he would be discovered; a deep desire to earn his true measure of punishment; a sly hope that somehow he would escape retribution again; a body-aching need to enjoy again and even more intensely the tenderness and warmth of physical contact.

He stood outside the door as he had done on that other night – was it last week or the week before? The corridor was blissfully dark and silent. There was a new, weak sliver of moon that night and no wind. The absence of noise was unusual. When he focused on that for a moment, it brought him back more fully to himself. He knew he should go back. This was wrong. He still had time. She would know nothing if he turned back now. There was no risk. There would be no retribution.

He turned and went back along the bare dusty corridor, bundling along like some driven animal. But something inside stopped him. He couldn't keep away from her. He knew that.

He hurried, breathing fast, back to her door. He twisted the white china door handle and threw the door open. Then, quite suddenly, he stopped.

The bed was empty. She wasn't there.

Nancy kept to the same routine that she had followed for over twenty years: going outside at five o'clock every afternoon, walking round the garden, pausing in the summer house and always, always, always ringing the bell. She didn't mind the bell: didn't even think much about it any more. If anything, she found it somehow reassuring – comforting almost. It seemed to have no weight. She lifted it and dropped it with no apparent effort, with no exercise of her will whatsoever. But now, when she was in the garden, she looked around her more than ever before. She saw as if for the first time how neglected both the house and the garden had become. She would look for the girl at the windows. Sometimes she would catch sight of her, most often at that little window in the half-basement where the kitchen was. They would, of course, make no sign to each other. They had agreed that between themselves.

She would look up at her brother's bedroom window. But the curtains were always closed and she never saw him. She had only caught sight of him a few times over the years and each time she had always been surprised at how old he looked. She still remembered him most clearly as the serious, intense but affectionate young man that he had been when he went off to university, before her incarceration.

Nancy did her best to continue as normal. But she wondered how things could stay the same now that the girl was here. That concern – or fear – became more clearly defined for Nancy one night when she and the girl were sitting in the back room, eating cakes which Mrs Weir and Grace had baked that afternoon.

The radio was on as usual. A youngish-sounding

man with a comforting, easy English accent was reporting with great enthusiasm from America on films. Nancy had never been to a cinema. Grace had tried to explain what the experience was like to her but Nancy found the concept hard to grasp. It was then that Grace said, 'I could take ye tae one.'

There was a moment of silence as the implications of this settled between them. Grace seemed to be quite aware of what she had said and watched Nancy carefully to see her reaction.

'I couldnae do that.'

'Why no?'

'I couldnae leave here.'

'Ye could, ye know. It wouldnae be hard.'

'No.'

'Ye would like it.'

'James wouldnae let me.'

'If we didnae come back, it wouldnae matter.'

Nancy became agitated at this point.

'I don't understand.'

'We could stay together.'

'What?'

'Ye don't need to stay here. We could go away. Somewhere quite different. Just the two of us. Start all over again.'

'No. No. We couldnae.'

'Yes. We could.'

'What wid we dae?'

'Don't worry about that. I wid look after us.'

'No. I couldnae leave here.'

'How no?'

'Please. I jist couldnae.'

The girl waited while Nancy became calmer. The same voice continued on the radio, now talking about an election. She put her hands over Nancy's.

'Why d'ye think I came here?'

'I don't know.'

'Ye don't think it was jist an accident? A coincidence?'

After a moment, Nancy shook her head.

'I came here tae get ye and take ye away from here. That's the only reason I'm here.'

Nancy shook her head. She couldn't do that. The very thought filled her with heart-stopping panic. She couldn't ever go away from here. She couldn't remember what else was said that night. But she knew, in her heart, that this was only what she had expected from the girl.

It was as if she had already known this was what the girl would say – and was what she had come for – the first time she had appeared in these rooms.

Time was a blur for Renwick. But it seemed to him that it was several nights later that he heard a noise from the floor above him. There was the creak of a floorboard. Then footsteps, very light, on the stairs.

The noise was almost imperceptible. For seconds, it vanished altogether so that he wondered if he had only imagined it. Then it was back again

– light, faint, but definitely there. Feet on the stairs. He was sure of it. Her feet. Coming down from the attic. Onto the landing a few feet away from the door of the study where he was standing, behind the door, listening.

There was another pause – or hesitation? He waited. He heard the steps again, on the half-flight of stairs which ran to the back of the house and turned under the stained glass window to go down to the main hall and front door.

He'd opened the door of the study by this time.

The footsteps continued down to the main hall. He moved along the corridor, keeping close to the wall where the floorboards were less likely to creak under him. He heard the girl – he knew it was her – go down the last few steps and move across the hall. He reached the half-landing just in time to see her disappearing between the curtains that led to Nancy's room. There was the rustling and turning of a key in a lock. A door opened and closed, the sound muffled by the heavy velvet curtains.

Renwick sat on one of the bottom steps, in the darkness, leaning his head against the cold stone wall. After a time, he could hear something else.

The sound of two women talking.

Grace continued to press Nancy on the subject of leaving.

She wasn't insistent or hysterical. Quite the opposite, in fact. Sometimes a whole night or two would pass without any mention of the subject. But Nancy felt that it was never very far away.

They would find themselves coming back to it, easily, almost by accident it seemed. Grace must have known that any other approach would have frozen Nancy with fear and turned her completely against the idea. Whenever the talk did turn to leaving, Nancy was adamant that she wouldn't go. She told Grace, quite simply, that she couldn't do it. She couldn't imagine life outside the house, outside these rooms and the walled garden. There was safety and security here. This had been the only world she had known for over twenty years. It terrified her to think of what life might be like out there in the real world. There would be other people to deal with. People who would talk to her and expect her to talk back. There would be decisions to make. There would be danger. Where would they live? What would they do? Could she cope with other people? Could she manage – now – to walk down a street, even here in the village, or go into a shop and buy things, with money?

No, it was easier and more comfortable to stay here. This life, curiously enough, had advantages – something she had never thought about before. But then she'd had no cause to think about these things before.

One night, Grace cut Nancy's hair. Nancy was quite shocked when she first saw it. She had let her hair grow over the years, taking a little off it occasionally. Now Grace had cut into a straight, rather severe line on the level with the lobes of her ears. The style was similar to Grace's own though not quite as short. It made her look younger. Nancy could see that. And, as the days passed, she grew to like it.

It was much the same with the make-up which Grace tried on her. She used very little – a touch of lipstick and some gentle dabbing with a pencil to accentuate the eyebrows and shape of the eyes.

Grace also helped her make some new clothes. They cut and stitched new dresses and blouses and skirts – a whole new wardrobe, in fact. Nancy would try them on at various stages, with a kind of flustered excitement that made her seem younger than her years. Grace took pleasure in her pleasure. They chattered and laughed together as they worked, easy in each other's company. The two women would discuss the adjustments or the length of a hem just like any two women anywhere in the country. Nancy often said – in her talks with the psychiatrists – that these were the best and happiest times of her life.

Whenever they did discuss leaving, they would go through the same ritual. Nancy would say no. Grace would push her but only a little. If the subject began to distress Nancy, Grace would drop it and move on to something else.

But through it all, Nancy knew what Grace was doing with the hair and the make-up and the

125

clothes. She was preparing Nancy for the world. And, despite the fact that Nancy continued to reject the idea, she knew in her heart that she was beginning to come round to it.

He was waiting for her at the top of the stairs.

He had no idea how long he'd waited there. At first he'd thought he should go straight in, confront both of them. But he didn't know how he would have dealt with his sister. It would be easier to tackle the girl on her own.

He climbed upstairs to the top floor of the house and found a room near the head of the stairs. He sat on the bare wooden floor, his back against the wall, with the door open so that he would see her as she came up. The room was dark and stripped of its furniture, apart from some chairs jumbled together under the window. But he knew which room it was. He remembered a maid, Agnes Breen, who had lived in this room when he and Nancy were young. She had always been good to them, told them stories, gave them sweets (forbidden by their parents). Above all, she gave them her affection and love. This room at the head of the stairs was a refuge. A place to come for comfort. He wondered what had happened to Agnes Breen. He couldn't remember her leaving – simply a time when she was here and then a time when she wasn't.

He heard the footsteps again.

She was on the flight below, coming up. There

was just the merest noise. But he knew it was her. He rose to his feet, still unsure of what he was going to say or do, still in his heart frightened of the girl and yet drawn to her. He was angry at her – for what she had done to him and his life. She had turned everything on its head, shredded the fabric of his daily life like some infernal machine. But the fear was there, too. The fear was always there now.

She came up the last few stairs quickly. Her head was bent forward so that she could keep her eyes on where she was going. She had what looked like a piece of material in one hand and some wooden bobbins of thread in the other. He let her go by the door. She didn't see him. Didn't even look in his direction.

She started along the bare, deep-shadowed corridor. It was then that he swung out and grabbed her. She screamed and fell against the wall, trying to escape from him. He lost his grip on her arm as she fell. She scrabbled away from him, along the floor, then rose and started running along the corridor, crying. She dropped the material and the thread. He tore after her, banging against the corridor walls as if he were too big to be contained in this space.

She reached her room and slammed the door shut. He jammed his foot in the door just before it closed and he threw his weight against it, sending it flying open and the girl sprawling across the floor. Her dress flew up, revealing white thighs above her stockings and grey underwear. She was smiling at him. She made no attempt to close her legs. That, anyway, is what he said.

He woke up, lying on the floor.

She was sitting on the chair, watching him. She was wearing a dressing gown.

She wasn't afraid of him. Renwick thought he had hit her. He distinctly remembered trying to make her lie still with a blow from his fist. There was no mark on her face. She was combing out her hair, looking down at him with that half-smile still playing on her lips.

'I want ye outa here,' he said, trying to sound authoritative. 'First thing in the mornin.'

She shook her head.

'I'll leave soon. But no just yet.'

'Who are ye? What do ye want here?'

She went on combing her hair for several moments. Then she laid down the brush and turned to him.

'I was born on the third of March, 1911. In this house. The midwife that took the child away was called Lizzie Baird. She came frae Paisley and was hired by yir faither for twenty-five pounds.'

He tried to say something but his voice was so weak he hardly made a sound.

'I'm Nancy's daughter.'

'Naw. Nancy doesnae huv a daughter.'

'No. Ye don't know what Nancy had, do ye? No one ever knew that. No even Nancy.'

128

'I'm no listenin tae this. I want ye gone. In the mornin. I'll gie ye money. I don't want to ever see ye again.'

'I'm no ready tae go.'

'If ye don't go first thing, ye won't get a penny.'

'I don't want money.'

Renwick shook his head. This couldn't be happening to him. It couldn't.

'How could I know these things if they werenae true? Naebody in this village knew what happened tae Nancy or her child. Lizzie Baird was the only person who knew anythin. She wis supposed tae take me fae here tae the Quarrier's Homes at Bridge i' Weir. Tell them nothin about me. And never see me again.'

Renwick stepped out of the room, backing away from her. The girl continued to talk quietly, watching him. She came after him, following him down the corridor and standing at the top of the stairs as he stumbled down, desperate to get away from her.

'Lizzie wis fond of me, though. Kept me at her ain hoose, in Newton St, in the West End of Paisley, for two years. Then she had tae take her ain mother into the hoose an care for her. It was only then I went to Quarrier's. But she still came tae visit me every month. She told me everythin about where I had come fae and what had happened tae me. Lizzie died when I was twelve.'

Renwick shook his head. 'If this is true, why did ye come here?'

'I came for my mother.'

'No.' Renwick was feeling confused and dizzy. The girl was slipping away from in front of him. He said that she was disappearing, literally, into thin air as she spoke.

'An I came to punish the people who did this to my mother. Kept her here like somethin less than human.'

'I didnae do anythin.'

'Ye let it be done. And never lifted a finger to help her. No one in this whole damn village did.'

Her presence became fainter and fainter until she was no longer there. He was sure he was imagining this. He knew he was ill, perhaps with some sort of fever. That was why everything seemed so strange to him. Now, he was standing on the stairs, completely alone, with her words ringing out around him. He could smell something, too, something unutterably sharp and acrid. It hung in the air, burning his nostrils and making him retch. He listened for her and looked along the corridor but the girl had gone, absolutely gone.

Eight

He was surprised that nothing had happened. He thought the girl would go straight to Mrs Weir. Then she might send Simmie in to see him or, more likely, pack him off in the car to fetch the police. He was sure he would have heard the car go off. But there had been nothing – not yet anyway. He remembered back to when he was a child and he'd wait like this for his father to punish him. It was better, always better, to have it over with. The pain of being hit was never as agonizing as the waiting. You never knew when he would come. Sometimes he would follow you upstairs. Other times he would leave it for hours. Always, the first you knew was the sound of the footsteps coming up the stairs. You would already be crying before the door opened.

He must have drifted off again. When he woke,

damp with sweat, shivering, the room was
brighter. This was puzzling and disturbing. But
there was something else. Oh yes, he could hear it
now. And he knew what it was. It was the sound
of footsteps coming up the stairs.

When Mrs Weir came into the kitchen that morning, she couldn't see the girl. The fire had been
cleaned out and stoked up again in the range. The
trays for the Master and Mistress were laid out on
the large well-scrubbed table. There was no food
or pots of tea on them as yet: they wouldn't
normally do that until just before they were due to
go upstairs at seven-thirty.

It was odd, Mrs Weir thought, but the house
seemed quieter than usual. She was somehow
very aware of the noise her shoes made as she
scuffled across the cold stone floor of the kitchen
and went into the hall. She stood there, looking
up the dark well of the stairway.

'Grace?' She called the name softly. There was
no answer.

'Grace? Ye up there?'

She kept her voice low but she was fairly sure
the girl would have heard her, if she'd been
there.

Mrs Weir eased the poker into the coals in the
fire, opening them to the air. A shower of sparks,
coal dust igniting, scattered up the chimney and
almost instantly flames began to quiver into life
just below the surface of the coals. Mrs Weir set

the kettle on the range and began the process of organizing breakfast.

She made the first pot of tea and the girl still hadn't returned. Mrs Weir was pretty sure she was out in the washroom. This was a small, separate building next to the lawn at the side of the house which they used as a washing green. There had been some sheets to be done: she was probably working her way through that and had forgotten the time. Mrs Weir had to see Renwick that morning. Generally, at this time of year, they bought a carcass of beef from Watson the butcher, in Lochwinnoch. Simmie had tried to order it on the Saturday but Watson wouldn't take the order because of the amount Renwick owed him. Mrs Weir didn't look forward to telling Renwick this but the chances were he'd just write her a cheque there and then without comment. He was rarely difficult about such things.

The girl still hadn't returned by the time Mrs Weir had the breakfasts ready so she decided to take the Master's up herself and she could deal with the business of Watson at the same time. When she was going along the corridor to his room, Mrs Weir heard a door close downstairs. That was probably Grace, she thought. There was no point in calling her up now. She knocked on the study door. There was no answer. She balanced the tray on one hand and opened the door with the other.

She saw him instantly. He was sitting on the

floor, backed up against a chair. He seemed to be consumed with fear. He still had yesterday's clothes on and had clearly been sitting there all night. He was speaking to her but she couldn't understand what he was talking about. He implored her not to be hard on him. Asked her not to get the police. He would pay. He could pay. It wasn't his fault. He didn't mean it. He kept asking about the girl, wanting to know if she was all right. Mrs Weir was suddenly worried for the girl. She wondered if he had done something to her: she was appalled by how quickly and easily the thought came to her.

She tried to get him up onto the chair but she couldn't move him on her own.

'Simmie! Grace! Whoever's doon there, can ye come up quick.'

He was holding onto her now, as if he didn't want to let her go. It was all she could do to stay on her feet. After a moment, someone else came in behind her. She turned and saw it was the girl. Mrs Weir was relieved to see that there was nothing wrong with Grace. Her sleeves were rolled up and a little wet from the washing, which is obviously what she had been doing.

'I'm sorry, Mrs Weir. I forgot the time. Whit's wrong?'

'I don't know. He's got some sort o' fever.'

For the moment, Renwick had gone still. He released Mrs Weir and stared at the girl. Suddenly, he tried to stand. He went towards the girl and then, slowly, he backed away from her, as if he were somehow afraid of her. He was very unsteady on his feet and quite incoherent by now and Mrs Weir wasn't surprised when he collapsed on the floor in front of them.

He didn't move. She put her hands to his mouth and felt his breath.

'Get Simmie an we'll get him intae bed. God knows whit's the maitter wi him.'

'Are we goin tae get the doctor?'

'He wouldnae thank ye for that.'

But Mrs Weir wasn't sure. She had never seen him like this before. Maybe she ought to risk his wrath. She'd see what Simmie said.

'Let's wait and see.'

The girl brought Simmie in. Between them, the three of them carried and dragged Renwick through to his bed. They laid him there and took off most of his clothes. Mrs Weir bathed his face and made him as comfortable as she could. Then they left him to sleep.

Somehow, the blow hadn't landed.

That had never happened to him in his life before. And he couldn't understand why.

There wasn't a mark on the girl. Not a bruise, nor a cut, nor a graze. But it was more than just that. It had been her manner, the way she looked, everything about her — it had all been quite normal. There was no hesitation or sense of fear as she came into the room: he registered that quite clearly. Her sleeves were rolled up and the arms of her blouse were wet here and there as if she'd just, until a few moments before, been washing clothes. It was as if the previous night had never happened. He hadn't been able to take this on board at the time but it was all utterly clear to him now, as he lay in bed in the early afternoon.

Mrs Weir had been up to see him twice. Her manner had been solicitous, concerned. She even broached the subject of a doctor, which he dismissed out of hand.

After her second visit, he asked to be left alone for a while to rest. He listened to her go downstairs, waited a few moments then got out of bed. He wrapped a dressing gown round him and made his way carefully along the corridor and upstairs.

There was not a thing out of place in the girl's room. The bed was made. The drawers were tidily closed. She had a few personal items – a brush, a cheap bottle of eau de Cologne, a small pair of nail scissors and so forth – arranged quite precisely on top of the drawers. The window was slightly open to let in fresh air. The curtains were neatly pulled back. Renwick looked at the pillow and the sheet. There had been blood, from when he hit her across the face: he could see the image in his mind now and it sickened him. He wondered about last night and how, even afterwards, he had been surprised there seemed to be no marks on her face. It had been dark though, and he wasn't thinking straight or seeing clearly. There was no blood anywhere on the crisp clean cotton sheets. She could have changed these, but why would she have done that? It was the same quilt. He was sure of that. No blood. Nor could he see any on the blankets. The chair. It stood at the side of her bed and some of her clothes had been folded on it. He had heard it smash as he had struggled to hold her down. The chair was there. There was no damage to it, none at all. He got down on his hands and knees to look on the carpet for any fragments of wood which she might have missed. There was nothing. The chair, the floor, the whole room – everything was just as it should be.

Mrs Weir began to take his meals up to Renwick again because the girl seemed to upset him now. According to Mrs Weir, Grace dealt with his strange behaviour well: it clearly disturbed her but she made a real effort not to let this show too much.

Renwick stayed in his study and still, she thought, looked none too well. She wasn't sure what he did there all day but she didn't think he was working, not as he had done before. There were papers and books on his desk but sometimes they were the same ones, in the same place, for several days. Once she suggested that they call in the doctor. He suddenly became quite animated and aggressive: he absolutely forbade her from contacting the doctor. Otherwise, he hardly spoke to her.

On the following Saturday evening, she asked him if he would want the car the following day. If he did Simmie would get it ready and leave it in front of the house as usual. He didn't answer her. Mrs Weir felt somehow, perhaps for the first time ever, sorry for him. She told Simmie he'd better get the car ready anyway, just in case.

The car was still there, standing black and silent, when they got up on the Sunday morning. That wasn't totally unusual. The time at which he left depended on where he was preaching. If he was preaching in Paisley or Glasgow he wouldn't need to leave until mid morning. When she took his breakfast up to him, she asked about the car. All he did was look at her with a kind of terror in his eyes.

It was then that she knew they wouldn't be in the house for very much longer. Simmie didn't disagree with her when she told him this. They'd thought they had the job and the cottage for life. Neither of them could face going back to the squalor and poverty of Glasgow. But somehow, after that Sunday, it became a very real prospect. Mrs Weir tried to keep these fears from the girl and shelter her generally from the oddness of Renwick's behaviour. She didn't want the girl to leave. Also, quite simply, she wanted to shield the girl from any unpleasantness, just as she would have done with any young or innocent person.

A Child of Air

On the Tuesday or Wednesday of that second week, she sent Simmie up to see him on the pretext that something needed doing to the car. But Simmie could get nothing out of him and had no more idea of what was troubling him than Mrs Weir herself.

The Weirs were wakened soon after five o'clock by someone hammering on the door of their cottage. When Simmie opened the door, he found Renwick standing in front of him.

'Keys.'

That was all he said. He looked exhausted, dark-eyed and burnt-out, like a man balanced on the very edge.

'Whit, Sir? I'm sorry. I didnae catch that.'

'For the . . . the car.'

It took a moment for this to sink in with Simmie. By that time, his wife was standing beside him, capably taking things in hand as she wrapped her dressing gown round her.

'Fetch the keys for the car, Simmie.'

She was disturbed by the Master's appearance but she wasn't afraid to quiz him as Simmie went through to the kitchen for the keys.

'Where wid ye be goin, Sir?'

'Paisley. Maybe Glasgow. I don't know.'

'Wid ye no wait and have some breakfast, Sir. I could make ye somethin. Wouldnae take long.'

She was genuinely concerned about him. She wondered if she might even be able to dissuade him from going if she could just get him to sit down in her kitchen and talk to her.

'No. I need tae go now. Simmie! Where are they keys?' Simmie came hurrying back and gave him the keys. 'I'll come and gie ye a hand to get the engine startet.'

'I can manage.'

He had already turned and was stumbling away from them towards the garage. Mrs Weir ran after him.

'When will ye be back, Sir?'

'I don't know.'

'Will it be the day. Or tomorrow. Or—'

He didn't answer her. She stopped following him and came back to stand close beside Simmie. They watched as he threw open the garage doors and, a few moments later, drove away in the car, leaving the garage doors wide open behind him.

The night before he left Renwick had gone downstairs to a storeroom which was on the same level as the kitchen. This room ran towards the front of the house, under the hall, and had no window. No one had been in here for years. It had been used to store all manner of things – books, tools, linen which was kept in well-made wooden chests, cutlery and sets of china dishes, all of which had been used when the house was run by Old Man Renwick and it had bustled with life. Now, of course, there was no need for any of these things. Down here, too, were kept his father's and grandfather's papers and all the account books for the house dating back to the middle of the last century. Until the last week or so, Renwick had kept up the annual account book for the house, entering each debit and each credit with the same scrupulous precision.

The account books were stored in metal boxes. They had been packed away carefully each year by Renwick or his father or some long-forgotten factor. Year by year, they were all there. It didn't take him long to find the book for 1911. The vellum covers had been badly damaged and warped by damp. The pages were stuck together here and there but with care he could prise them open. The writing was his father's – broad, angular strokes of black ink that had greyed with time. He turned to March – a new month, a new set of pages. There was nothing. No debit of £25. No mention of a Lizzie Baird. The girl had been lying then. She'd made it all up – cleverly, cunningly – so that it sounded convincing. The details were what had made the difference. She had been skilful in her use of specifics. That was what had lent credence to her story.

Renwick's confidence was short-lived, however. He couldn't understand why there was no mention of the expense of Nancy's confinement. His father had recorded everything – but then would he have recorded this? Would he have disguised it under some other heading? He went through each of the entries for March individually. There was nothing out of the ordinary. There was no debit of £25. He turned to April but found nothing there either. In the pages for May, he came across an entry which stopped him. It was for the sum of £33 14s 6d, paid to Messrs Abercrombie, 33 Jamaica St, Glasgow. It was entered under 'Personal Expenses'. All it said was 'in payment of invoice'. Every other entry was itemized. Not this one. He felt, with sinking heart, that this was the entry he'd been looking for. It was when he saw that, that he knew he would have to leave, have to go and prove that the girl had been lying for himself. Prove it beyond any doubt.

At the Registrar of Births and Deaths in Paisley, behind the station, it took him some time to track down a death certificate for an Elizabeth Baird. The cause of death was given as 'Heart Failure'. The address was 22 Newton Street. The girl had mentioned 'Newton Street' but that could just be another of those clever, persuasive details. The girl could well have known a Lizzie Baird who lived in Newton Street but that didn't mean she was Nancy's daughter. Renwick reminded himself that neither he nor anyone else even knew what sex Nancy's child had been. The child could just as easily have been a boy as a girl.

Newton Street was different from all the other

streets around it. They had tenements on both sides, crowding in on the pavements, shutting out the sky. Newton Street had tenements along only one side. On the other, there was a small, carefully laid-out park with tree-lined paths, trimmed lawns, flower beds, a bowling green surrounded by a squared-off privet hedge and a bandstand. It was almost as if this was the front garden for the tenements on the other side of the road and, certainly, the children from the tenements used it as such. The reason for this rare luxury of greenery and space was that the land was owned by the Coats Thread Company. The main entrance of their factory – a pair of vast and vastly self-important wrought iron gates – stood at the top of Newton Street.

Renwick found an old woman, on the second floor at number 22, who remembered Lizzie Baird. She introduced herself as Miss White and was rather better spoken than Renwick would have expected to find here. Lizzie Baird had lived in the flat opposite, the old woman told him. No, she couldn't remember any child living there but then Lizzie had been there before she arrived. She knew Lizzie had had a married sister. Her first name had been Elspeth and she had been a nurse like her sister. Miss White believed she had worked at the TB hospital in Elderslie – well, at least, she did the last time Miss White had heard, which would have been five or six years ago.

* * *

Renwick felt better after talking to Miss White. He decided he would leave Lizzie Baird's sister for the time being and find out about Messrs Abercrombie.

He parked the car facing down to the river by the toilets in Clyde Street. It was six o'clock. He heard the clock in St Enoch Square chime out the hour. He was prepared to find no trace of Messrs Abercrombie at number 33. If that's what he found, then there were ways of checking what sort of company it had been through old business directories. He could find those at the Mitchell Library.

Number 33 was a close between a shoe shop and one of the city's less glamorous cinemas. There were plaques and metal signs up and down each side of the doorway. And there, among them, was a small green plaque which said:

The Abercrombie Agency
3rd Floor

He took the lift up. There were several doors facing him when the lift stopped. None of them were for the Abercrombie Agency. He slid open the gate of the lift and stepped out. Abercrombie's was the last door he came to, half-hidden in a blind corridor. The door was frosted glass in a dark-stained, wood surround. There was no light

on inside. On the door, in black Gothic script, he
could read:

The Abercrombie Agency
Nurses, Medical Staff &
Companions to the Elderly

He tried the door. It was locked and there was no
one inside.

It was on the first night of Renwick's absence that
Ferguson had his accident.

There are two accounts of this accident, both
given by Ferguson, but given at different times in
his life. This is the account which he gave at the
time of the accident.

He was in the wood up behind the village hall.
He was going round the snares he'd laid: he was
always after badgers and foxes because you could
sell the skins. And, besides, he enjoyed hunting
and killing animals, even those which wouldn't
provide you with any food.

It wasn't easy to see your snares up there, or to
remember exactly where they were. So he went
carefully, listening for the slightest of noises and
trying to locate the snares by the landmarks of a
distinctive tree or a particular rock.

Suddenly, he heard the noise of a largish animal struggling under the ferns. He assumed it
must be caught in one of his snares, probably
exhausted by its attempts to get free and panicked

147

into movement again by his presence.

He didn't remember leaving a snare there but it was dark and, besides, animals could move snares, even if they were pegged down.

He couldn't see what it was. It would struggle, squeal, shake the ferns and then lie silent again. Whatever it was, it was a fair size and still had plenty of fight left in it.

He went closer. It was snarling and hissing. He tried to shut his eyes a little in order to focus better on what might be in there. But it was no good. The animal was trapped under quite tall, dense maidenhair ferns.

He leaned forward cautiously. He poked his stick in and lifted aside some of the ferns. All he saw was a glimpse of fur and something white. But it was all so brief, over before he had a chance to register whether it was a fox as he thought.

The animal retreated even deeper into the ferns. He leaned forward again. Closer this time. It was then that the animal came flying at him. He didn't know what it was. There wasn't time to see anything. Claws sank into his face and tore at his eyes and skin.

He screamed and fell back, fighting to haul the animal off. He could feel its fur and smell its rank, nauseous breath right against his mouth. It spat and snarled, tearing at him again and again.

Then it was gone. But he was still screaming.

There were still a few people in the village hall and they heard him. No one knew who it was or

why anyone should be up there: it wasn't
Ferguson's land up there but then that wouldn't
stop him taking anything from there if he could
find it.

A couple of the men went up to the woods and
found Ferguson stumbling around. He was holding his hands to his face but the blood was
streaming from between his fingers. He told them
– though he wasn't very coherent – that it was a
wildcat.

That made sense. In fact, it was the only
explanation that would have made sense to
them. A wildcat protecting her young. He
thought he had her in a snare but the reason she
wouldn't move was that she had young there.
Some of the men went up into the woods the
day afterwards to find and kill her. But they
couldn't see any trace of a den. They could tell
where it had happened. The ferns were flat-
tened and broken and there was blood smeared
on the leaves and the rocks and the trees. It was
strange. They should have been able to find
feathers and bones of the small animals the cat
had eaten. There was nothing.

Someone fetched a car and took Ferguson to
hospital. He was away for several months. He lost
the use of his sight completely. When he came
back, his face was a mass of scars which would
never heal. He had lost part of his nose and lips
and in those days there was little that could be
done for such injuries. He couldn't run the farm

anymore. A distant, unmarried, female cousin came to look after him.

People got used to seeing him around the village though he was always a figure of fear to the younger children. He would sit in Innes' Bar for hours at a time, no one talking to him, waiting for the cousin or someone else to walk him back up to the farm. He was certainly, people said, a changed man. Ferguson had never been liked so there was little, if any, real sympathy for him. Besides, life was hard and people had their own troubles to deal with. No one had it easy. Not up there anyway.

After a few years he stopped coming down to the village. And most people in the village forgot about him. He lived on in his farmhouse with the distant, unmarried cousin until he died in 1971. Several years after the accident, Ferguson gave another account of what happened that night.

Ferguson said he had been hanging around the village hall for weeks before that night. Every night he would take a turn up there. Mostly he kept to the wood behind the village hall. Yes, he could trap things up there. But that wasn't why he was there. He was watching for Grace, waiting for his chance. That night he thought his luck was in when he saw her on her own coming down from the big house. She was carrying something, something in a box. He'd no idea what it was. He set a few more traps – there was a big badger set up there and he hadn't so far been able to catch even one of them. He waited patiently for her. He was in no hurry, no rush. It was a long way back up that road. He couldn't miss her.

He was waiting by the road, in among some trees, as she came up. She hadn't been long. He even wondered if maybe she'd seen him and was keen to lock horns, as it were. She didn't seem surprised when she saw him. She kept walking. He walked alongside her for a few moments, talking to her. She ignored him completely. That wasn't on. He stepped in front of her and blocked her path. She slipped away from him but he grabbed her and tried to kiss her.

As he did so, she bit his lip. Her teeth went clean through it. He yelled and jumped back, holding his mouth. She darted away into the trees.

After a moment, warm blood streaming down into his mouth, he was after her. Tearing through the trees. Stopping every so often to listen for her up ahead. She wouldn't escape him this time.

He could see her now. Running up ahead of him. He would catch her. He knew his way around here.

He edged up to the right where the ground rose. He knew she would come out to the little piece of flat ground near the waterfall. He arrived there just as she did, springing down at her from above when she thought he was still behind her.

The ground was covered with ferns, waist high

they were and even higher in places. The water
from the stream kept them moist and abundant.
She went rolling away from him as he jumped
down on her. He came wading after her, sweep-
ing the ferns aside. She scrambled away on all
fours underneath the fragile green canopy, looking for somewhere to hide.

He was right above her now, his feet just
behind hers. She curled herself into a ball. He
couldn't see her very clearly. He put one arm
down to her, reaching. She was sobbing. It was
the only sound in the forest. And then the sound
changed. It was no longer like crying. It was like a
panting, painful, as if something was struggling
to be born. Ferguson stopped, his hand just above
her. She was on him, somehow clamped to the top
of his body and slicing at his face and his eyes
with her claws or her nails.

He couldn't see a thing. He didn't feel what she
was doing to him. He was just trying to get away,
so terrified was he. There was a smell in the air,
too, a sudden piercing sulphurous smell. He was
trying to push her away as he stumbled over the
rough, boulder-strewn ground under the ferns.
He wanted to get her off. All he could remember
were glimpses of this dark shape fastened round
the top part of his body. When he touched her, he
could feel fur. He swore that he could feel some
kind of short stubby fur on her skin. The touch of
this terrified him even more. He fell over. She
stayed where she was and rolled over and over

with him, her nails tearing again and again into his face.

That was the last thing he could remember, rolling over and over through the ferns, screaming and trying to push her away from him. He was a strong man too, Ferguson, but he was utterly powerless to shift her.

Ferguson remembered nothing more until he woke up in hospital three days later, his face swathed in bandages and his eyes covered and unseeing.

The Weirs heard about Ferguson and the wildcat from Alec McAuley, the postman. They were appalled but their minds were, understandably, more focused on Renwick and their own immediate future.

They had been waiting for the storm to break for some time and it looked as if this was finally it. They had some money saved so they would be okay for a while at least. But they didn't know where they would go. They didn't actually want to go anywhere. They wanted to stay in the village but there would be no work for them and nowhere for them to live. If the big house closed down, as now seemed increasingly likely, there would be nothing else they could do. They weren't going back to Glasgow, on that point they were quite definite.

Mrs Weir tried to keep their concerns from the girl. Grace had been such a help to them and to her in particular. She was always willing to lend a hand and nothing was too much trouble for her. The night before, for instance, she had walked down to the village hall for Mrs Weir.

Mrs Weir had made a large fruit cake which one of the women, who was especially good at that sort of thing, was going to ice and decorate for the dance. Simmie would normally have taken Mrs Weir and the girl down in the car but Renwick had the car so they weren't sure what to do.

The girl had been quite happy to walk there and back in the darkness. Simmie offered to go with her but she said it wouldn't be necessary. Mrs Weir was just glad Grace had left the hall before Ferguson was found. She wouldn't have liked the girl to see him, not the way he must have looked.

Renwick spent the night in a sailors' hostel in one of the streets to the west of Jamaica Street. It was a damp, foul-smelling building – naked lights, uncarpeted floors, rooms that had been partitioned off from larger rooms. The sheets on his bed hadn't been changed and the bed hadn't been made but none of this mattered to Renwick. Nor did the insects that occasionally scuttled across the walls.

He kept the light on all night and sat on a hard upright chair by the window. He didn't want to sleep. He had more control over his terror when he was awake. At one point that night, a woman appeared in the street down below. She came walking up from the river. He couldn't see her clearly and she was quite far away. But he was sure it was her. He knew it was the girl. She had a cloak on, with a hood like Nancy's. She came slowly up the other side of the road, moving through the pools of light cast by the yellow lamps. She stopped directly across from him, under a lamp, and looked up at him. He dropped down below the window. And when he looked again, she had gone.

Renwick left the hostel as soon as it began to grow light. He walked down to the river and then, as the sun came up, wandered among the warehouses and docks. It gave him some comfort to be lost in the everyday bustle. There were large liners and cargo boats bound for ports on the other side of the world. There were much smaller boats – tramps and tiny puffers that would take a cargo down the river to Greenock or up into the Highlands and Islands, the sea still offering the easiest means of transport up there. Everywhere men were working, loading and unloading a bewildering variety of cargos. Renwick walked for miles, mesmerized by the energy of a major city going about the business of making its living.

It was after ten o'clock when he came back to Jamaica Street. 'Messrs Abercrombie' was two rooms at the back of the building. The first room, occupied by a secretary, had no window at all. The second room looked directly over the trains coming out of Central Station: the trains on the nearest rails were no more than ten or twelve feet away from the window and, when they passed, made conversation virtually impossible. Mae Abercrombie occupied the second room, settled solidly behind a large oak desk. She was a heavy, rather mannish woman, in her fifties: short steely grey hair, tweed suit, severe white blouse. Her nails were clipped to the quick. She wore no make-up and smoked constantly, using a short (yellowed) ivory cigarette holder. Renwick disliked her intensely on sight. He wondered briefly about the relationship between Mae Abercrombie and the sharp young woman in the first room who was her secretary. But this wasn't his concern. He wanted only one thing from her – the name of the woman who had been the midwife at the birth of his sister's child.

'I'm sorry. We wouldn't have records going back that far.'

Her accent was sharp, clear, anglicized – every syllable given its due. She studied him with distaste from behind her cigarette, the smoke drifting up around her. She wasn't frightened of him. She wasn't frightened of any man.

'I don't believe ye.'

'Well. I'm afraid it really doesn't matter what you believe, Mr Renwick. We do not have the records. And nothing is going to change that.'

'I need tae know about this.'

'That may be the case. And we would very

much like to help you. But it is a long time ago. We don't keep the records for any more than five or six years. We wouldn't have anywhere to store them.'

'Ye remember, don't ye?'

'We have so many clients, Mr Renwick, that I couldn't possibly remember one particular request for staff over twenty years ago.'

She was lying. Renwick knew that. He had seen something in her eyes as soon as he told her why he'd come.

'I want tae know who ye sent for that job.'

'I can't help.'

'You're lyin.'

'I'm afraid I really must ask you to leave, Mr Renwick. There is nothing we can do for you. Good day.'

'I'll go as soon as ye tell me exactly what I want tae know.'

She was about to repeat herself, even more strongly this time. Renwick was up on his feet. He knocked the cigarette holder out of her mouth. She tried to rise. He pushed her back into her chair and jammed her against the wall, tilting the chair backwards so that she was within an inch of toppling over. She was a strong woman but totally powerless to resist him because, as she said later, he was clearly mad.

'Tell me who ye sent.'

He had his hand on her throat. The scuffling and raised voices had brought the secretary

157

through. As soon as she saw what was happening, she rushed back to her own office and reached for the phone.

'Don't phone the police, Jeanette.'

The secretary stood there, with the phone, frozen for a moment. Miss Abercrombie nodded to Renwick and he released her.

'Close the door, please, Jeanette. It's all right.' The secretary did as she was told. Renwick stayed on his feet, waiting. Miss Abercrombie lit a cigarette and drew deeply on it, not bothering now with the holder.

'Yes, I remember that job. We get some strange requests in this place but not many like that.'

'Ye supplied the midwife then? That would be whit the bill was for?'

'Yes.'

'Whit wis her name?'

'There would only be one person I could have sent on a job like that.'

'Who?'

'Lizzie Baird.'

Renwick drove straight into Elderslie. The TB hospital was a series of low buildings on a rise above the Paisley–Johnstone road. It was, and remained for years, both a TB sanatorium and a maternity hospital – an odd combination but one which clearly suited the medical authorities. He was lucky to find Lizzie Baird's sister on duty. To his surprise, she agreed to talk to him. He had decided, before he even met her, that money might be his most persuasive argument here. But she wouldn't touch his money. Left it lying on the table of the office where they spoke. It was the look in his eyes that made her decide to talk to him. It was a hunted, tormented look. She felt sorry for him but she also wanted to take the opportunity to hurt him even more: she felt that anyone connected with that family deserved whatever they had coming to them.

'Whit dae ye want tae know?' Her married name was Laing. She was a small, thin woman with brown hair and sad blue eyes.

'Yir sister was present when a child was born at Renwick House.'

'Aye. She wis.'

'What happened to the child?'

She didn't care what she said to him or how he reacted. She made no attempt to alter the facts.

'She brought it back tae Paisley.'

'Wis it a boy or a girl?'

'A girl.'

'Whit did she call it?'

'Grace. Grace Johnson.'

'Why Johnson?'

'That wis our mother's maiden name.'

'Was its birth ever registered?'

'Her birth. No as far as I know.'

'Why did yir sister keep the child?'

'She'd made up her mind before she even came

159

back. She didnae want tae abandon the child, like she was supposed tae.'

'How did she manage? It couldnae have been easy for her.'

'We all helped. My mother, me, friends. She wis a loveable wee thing, Grace. Everybody liked her.'

'Why did Lizzie gie her up?'

'My mother took a stroke.'

'When?'

'Maybe when Grace was two or three.'

Renwick nodded dully. He said nothing for a good few moments. Mrs Laing continued, taking the story to its natural conclusion.

'Lizzie tried tae keep the wean. She stopped working for a time and had both of them tae look after in that one-room flat. Ma ain first wean had jist been born so I couldnae dae much. And we had nae room tae take my mother. Lizzie was heart-broken at havin' tae gie up the wean. She found someone who could get her intae Quarrier's so that's what she did. Lizzie went tae see the lassie every month. She was so fond o that girl, I cannae tell ye. Far as I know, Lizzie went on visitin the girl every month till she died.'

'When was that?'

'Eight, nine year ago.'

'Did ye ever see the girl again?'

'No.'

'So ye wouldnae know what she looked like now?'

'No.'

160

Renwick sat for a moment in silence. Then he rose and left without saying another word. The money was still lying on the table. She gathered it up and walked down to the boilerhouse. There was a small auxiliary furnace which they used for burning swabs and bandages. She lifted the lid and dropped the money inside, not even pausing to see it burn.

Nancy didn't see Grace the first night Renwick was away, which was also the night of Ferguson's accident.

She was upset. It was the first time in a month that she hadn't had a visit from the girl. She gave up waiting at midnight. The radio had gone off and she disliked sitting there in the empty rooms on her own. She didn't sleep very well that night and all the next day she could only wonder if the girl would ever come back? What if she'd already gone, left without her?

It wasn't till the afternoon that she saw her. Grace was taking a straw basket of washing round to the green at the side of the house. She hoped the girl would look over at her window. But she didn't, though they had always agreed there would be no communication between them outside these rooms.

The girl arrived earlier than usual that second night. She apologized for the previous night and said she'd had to run an errand for Mrs Weir. Nancy asked her about James. She'd sensed that

161

he was away before the girl told her. Grace told her that he had some business to attend to in Glasgow and Paisley. That's all he was doing. No, she didn't know what kind of business.

The girl was excited. She had a bag in one hand, a kind of brown leather satchel. And she said, 'I've got somethin I want tae show ye.'

'What?'

'It's in here.'

'What is it? Is it a present?'

'Kind of.'

Nancy was intrigued. But Grace kept the satchel close to her chest for the moment, girlishly teasing her.

Nancy tried to guess what might be in it – papers, one of these phonograph records Grace had told her about, photographs, clothes. Grace, shaking her head and laughing, put the satchel on the dining table and opened it.

'Look inside.'

There was money in the satchel. Pound notes gathered together in bundles and wrapped in thick brown elastic bands.

'Where did ye get this?'

'I've been saving. It's for us.'

'I can't take this.'

'Of course ye can. Ye're my mother. Who else wid I share it wi'?'

Nancy put the money back in the satchel.

'That's enough for us tae live on. For a long time anyway. We'll get well away fae here. Start all over.

162

'No one would ever know who we were or where we'd come frae. Just a mother and daughter, that's all anyone would know. We would manage. We'll get a house. I'll show ye how to go shoppin – what tae buy, what tae say, what tae do with the money. We'll go tae the big shops up in Glasgow, or maybe we'll move tae Edinburgh. It's that bit further away. Maybe that would be better. We'll go tae the theatre, the pictures. We'll dae a' the ordinary things mothers and daughters usually dae.'

'I'm afraid.'

'There's nae need tae be. I'll be wi ye a' the time.'

After a moment, Grace said, 'Come o'er here.'

She was standing by the door that led out into the hall. 'Come here.'

Nancy stood up and went over to her. Grace turned the handle and opened the door. The second set of doors were lying open so she could see right out into the hall.

'Take my hand.'

Nancy did so. Instinctively, she turned to look at the bell.

'Ye don't need that.'

Grace led her through the first set of doors and into the hall. They stood there together for a few moments. Nancy looked around, taking it all in, crying quietly. It looked so small. This wasn't what she remembered – it had all been much bigger, much grander, far more intimidating.

They went through to the front room on the other side of the house. Everything here was more as Nancy remembered it, but again it was as if the sense of scale was missing. They went into the kitchen. Grace sat Nancy down at the kitchen table and made her a cup of tea. Nancy went over to the window over the sink.

'I see ye here sometimes.'

'Aye. I try to be there when ye're out. I was there the very first day I arrived here.'

'I know. I saw ye.'

The women drank their tea. Nancy kept running her fingers along the edge of the table, as if to reassure herself that it was real.

They were quiet for quite some time then Nancy said, 'I'll go.'

'What?'

'I'll go wi ye.'

'Good. That's good . . .'

'But I'm afraid.'

'Trust me.'

'When will we leave?'

'Tomorrow night.'

'Why no tonight?'

'Tomorrow's better. It's the night of the dance. Everybody will be busy wi that.'

That night, Grace slept with Nancy. She said it would be okay because there was no one else in the house. They fell asleep holding each other. In the morning, Grace was gone. There was no sign of her or the satchel. And the door was locked.

A Child of Air

★ ★ ★

It was pitch dark when Renwick turned the car out of the hospital gates and drove through Johnston. The main square was quiet, its flower beds neatly turned and cleared for the winter. He drove on, down a steep twisting hill, away from the lights again. There was a lace factory on one of the corners of this hill and, as Renwick came down, a driver was backing a lorry out of the despatch bay.

Renwick kept going at the same high speed and turned only at the last moment, crunching the side of his car along the back of the lorry. The impact sent him careering across the road. He went up onto the grass verge and almost into the wall on the other side of the road. Somehow, he managed to regain control of the car and get it back on the road. The driver of the lorry jumped from his cab and some of the men came running out of the yard. They saw Renwick's car swerve back onto the road just as a bus laboured up the hill from Houston. They said it was a miracle he wasn't killed.

Renwick lost his way several times that night. The roads on those moors were narrow and often untarred. Sometimes there would be signs at a crossroads and sometimes not, the roads only ever being used by locals who didn't need to be told where they were going. Even if there had been signs, Renwick was in no state to read them or follow them.

165

Around midnight, he found he had driven way past Quarrier's and come out on a quiet country road where the ground dropped suddenly and dramatically away in front of him. Below him, there was a mass of lights, blinking singly in the darkness. He didn't understand where he was at first. Then he realized these were the lights of Port Glasgow and Greenock. He stopped the car and got out. The lights stretched away to the west as far as he could see. Down by the river, there were brilliant pools of light around the hulls of ships that were being worked on all through the night.

Occasionally, there would be a sudden flare of sparks from one of the ships, silent, but perfectly visible even at this distance. On the river, there were lights moving slowly, smoothly – ships making their way up to Glasgow or down to the Tail of the Bank and beyond. On the other side of the river there were delicate strings of lights, barely visible, flickering weakly, which indicated small villages and the odd isolated house. As his eyes became accustomed to the darkness and the scale of what lay before him, he could pick out the heavy shapes of the mountains rising on the other side.

He stayed in the car all night, chilled, shaking with fever. Once again, he didn't allow himself to sleep.

Slowly, the dawn came in and the tracery of street lights beneath him lost its magic. Quite suddenly, the lights were extinguished in great patches and the streets just became ordinary streets again and the houses ordinary houses. Beyond the river, the mountains were a hazy peaceful blue.

Renwick reached The Quarrier's Homes soon after nine. The Homes were solid red sandstone buildings set in an expanse of neat lawn. There was a rather grand church at the end of the straight, smooth road that ran through the Homes. There were a few children about, less than he would have expected. Those that he saw were quite orderly, rather similarly dressed and all equally well-scrubbed.

He parked in front of the main office building. The Senior Clerk to whom he spoke said it was impossible for him to look at their records. The records were private. They could supply him with some information on the person concerned if he wrote to them and his application was approved by the Board of Directors of the Homes. This was usually just a formality but it did take several weeks, if not months. Renwick was desperate. He reminded the Clerk that his family had contributed handsomely to the building of The Homes and had set up a trust for them. The Clerk knew there was some connection to the family – he had recognized the name the instant Renwick introduced himself – but insisted that rules were rules. Renwick said the directors would be displeased to hear how he had been treated and he would make sure they heard all about it. This would be easy as his own solicitor, Carter, from Greenock, was on the Board. The man – his name was Cairns – was unsettled as much by Renwick's manner and intensity as by his threat. He didn't like Renwick and he wanted nothing more than to tell him to clear out of his office but, on the other hand, he couldn't afford to upset the directors. They were difficult, self-important meddlers at the best of times.

After a moment's deliberation, Cairns sent for the records. When they arrived, he refused to let Renwick see them. He would read through them and tell Renwick such information as he could.

Renwick wanted to meet the couple who had run the house in which Grace had lived. That wouldn't be possible, Cairns explained, as Mr and Mrs Cassidy had gone to work in a similar institution in Manchester. He could let Renwick have the address but Renwick was uninterested and said there was not enough time.

Cairns confirmed that Grace Johnson had arrived at the Homes at the age of two years and five months. Her next of kin was listed as Elizabeth Baird at the Newton Street address. He picked out some of the comments about Grace from the file – 'quiet and good-mannered', 'applies herself well to schoolwork and housework', 'an obliging child, always ready to lend a hand with the younger ones'. There were regular medical reports.

Cairns continued to leaf through the pages,

picking out a comment here and there. Then he stopped quite suddenly.

'Whit is it?'

'There must be some mistake.'

'What d'ye mean?'

'Ye say this girl works for ye?'

'Aye.'

'Then it cannae be this Grace Johnson.'

'Why no?'

'Because this Grace Johnson is deid.'

Renwick stared at him, stunned into silence.

'How did she die?'

'TB.'

'Are ye sure?'

'She passed away on the sixth October, 1925. She's buried in the cemetery behind the church out there.'

Nine

On the morning of the dance, Mrs Weir and Grace worked busily and happily in the kitchen. Mrs Weir knew that the times ahead were likely to be difficult. But, for today anyway, she would forget about the future and give herself up to the pleasures of the moment.

They had some scones and small cakes to bake: these were, of course, best done on the day. Then Mrs Weir tried on a few dresses to decide what she would wear that night. Several of the dresses, to their great amusement, no longer fitted her – and quite spectacularly so in one or two cases. The only one which did was a rather dowdy brown dress which both of them hated. The girl said they'd be better altering one of the others, which they proceeded to do. It was the girl who did most of the work and she made a good job of it. Even Simmie commented on how good the dress looked that evening – quite something, coming from Simmie. Mrs Weir felt that the girl was a little quieter and more tense than usual but she put this down to the Master's continued absence and the fact that the girl would probably sense how much this disturbed them.

The morning passed pleasantly. Even Grace seemed to brighten a little and forget her worries. It was about eleven-thirty when Simmie came into the kitchen where Mrs Weir was in her slip and the two women were giggling.

'There's a car comin up the road.'

'Is it the Master's?'

'No.'

'It's naeb'dy fae the village?'

'I don't recognize it.'

All three of them went through to the front room, the one that was still kept good. They could see the car. It was a small black Ford, not in the best of condition. It bumped and lurched up the unmade road, turning this way and that way as if trying to escape, but finding at every turn that what lay on either side was even less inviting. There were two people in the car. They couldn't see who they were.

The car came through the gate and followed the gravel driveway round to the steps of the front door. It stopped, the engine taking its time to die away completely.

The two people inside spoke for a few

moments. Mrs Weir could see their heads – just dark shapes behind the glass – turn to each other.

The driver stayed where he was. The passenger door swung open, kicking back on itself a little. It was a woman who got out of the car. Mrs Weir couldn't imagine who this might be. It was only when the woman turned to face the house that Mrs Weir saw it was Clair MacIndoe.

Mrs Weir gasped. Simmie shook his head.

'That's a' we need.'

The girl looked at them.

'Who is it?'

'Clair MacIndoe. Her that was the maid here afore you.'

'What do ye think she wants?'

'God only knows.'

Clair MacIndoe closed the car door. As she moved away from the car, they could see that the left sleeve of her coat was pinned up at the elbow.

'She cannae expect her job back anyway. No wi' that,' Simmie said.

She looked up at the house. Her face was thin. The last month or two had clearly taken a great deal out of her. Mrs Weir didn't like the look of this. It was trouble upon trouble but then wasn't that always the way of things?

'I'll talk tae her masel.'

'Ye're welcome. I'll be in the shed if ye need me.'

'Grace, you go oot an get the washin done. Stay oot there till she goes. Unless I call ye.' The girl nodded and did as she had been told.

Mrs Weir took Clair through to the kitchen. She had some water close to the boil, as usual, so she quickly made them some tea while Clair was still settling herself and looking around at the once-familiar room.

'I wis sorry tae hear about that.'

Mrs Weir nodded towards Clair's left arm.

'It wis either that or me. It very near wis me – for a time anyway.'

'Aye. I heard.'

'Ye get someone else?'

'Aye. A young lassie called Grace. She turned up just after – ah – that.'

'Ye were lucky.'

'I suppose we were. She's a good worker, too. Nice to have around.'

There was a moment or so of silence. Mrs Weir wondered if this had been the right thing to say as it clearly implied the opposite about Clair. Still, it was said and best left alone.

'The lassie likes it here, does she?'

'Seems to.'

Clair was looking at Mrs Weir in a way she didn't like.

'How does she get on wi his lordship?' Again, there was that look: a knowing smile, to which the lips barely gave expression.

'The lassie hardly ever sees him. She's never said much about him one way or the other.'

Mrs Weir knew very well, without wishing to

say it, what Clair MacIndoe was implying and was glad to see her disappointment, especially when she added, 'Apart from anythin, the Master's no been himsel this past few weeks. He's no gaun preachin. He's hardly been oot i his study.'

'Whit's wrong wi him?'

'Wish I knew. In fact, he's no even here now.'

'Where is he?'

'He went off three days ago. We've no seen him or heard from him since.'

Clair MacIndoe wasn't pleased to hear this.

'Why wid he dae that? He's naewhere tae go.'

Mrs Weir shook her head. She had nothing to offer by way of explanation.

'Tae tell ye the truth, I don't know that any i us'll be here much longer. That's what me and Simmie think anyway.'

Clair MacIndoe sat for a moment in silence. There was a kind of anger mixed with determination in her eyes.

Mrs Weir felt sorry for her. She had never much liked her but she wouldn't wish her situation on anyone.

'Whit are ye goin tae dae?'

'Well, I'm no about tae get a job, am I?' She lifted up the stump of her left arm.

'But I don't care. I've worked enough. I'm goin tae take things easy fae now on.'

There was an uncomfortable slyness in Clair MacIndoe's eyes. Mrs Weir wondered for a moment if the accident, or its aftermath, had affected her sanity.

'I want a word wi his lordship. Then I'll be OK.' Clair MacIndoe let the words hang in the air between them.

'I've nae idea whit ye're talking aboot, Clair. But it may be that the Master wid help ye.'

'Aye. It may be.' She didn't bother to hide the smile now, or conceal the heavy tone of sarcasm. And if Mrs Weir chose not to acknowledge what they were actually talking about, that didn't matter.

'Can I stay here, Jean?'

'No.'

Mrs Weir had been too quick with that.

'Big hoose like this.'

'The lassie's in yir room.'

'Nice.'

'Ye can have all yir stuff, if ye like. I've packed it away.'

'Mebbe another time.' She wasn't going to let Mrs Weir off so lightly. 'Plenty other rooms in the hoose.'

'I couldnae let ye stay here withoot the Master's permission. Ye ken that, Clair.'

Clair MacIndoe knew she couldn't get round that one, not in this house though, of course, she had no idea how things had changed in her absence. Still, she was angry at Mrs Weir. But then why should she expect anyone else to help her. She was going to help herself. Handsomely.

178

'When did ye come out of hospital?'

'Yesterday.'

'Where ye stayin?'

'I've taken a room in Greenock. But I don't expect tae be there for long.'

'I hope things work out for ye.'

'They will. Don't worry.'

Clair MacIndoe left the house at about one o'clock. Mrs Weir heard that Clair and her driver had stopped off at Innes's for a drink. No woman in the village would ever go in there – and Clair wouldn't have done so previously – but that didn't seem to bother her now. They stayed there well into the afternoon, drinking mostly by themselves but occasionally talking to Innes. She mentioned how keen she was to have a word with Renwick. She was interested to hear it was the night of the village dance, said she might even turn up.

They were still there when Renwick drove through the village some time after three. Innes asked her if she was going to go back up to the big house. She said no, she'd catch up with Renwick some other time. She and the driver finished their drinks and left, heading towards Greenock.

There had been a time – he could admit it to himself now – when he believed the girl might be Nancy's daughter. She had been so slyly convincing. She had driven him almost to the point of insanity when he believed that. It had been, literally, unbearable.

He remembered – with impunity now that he knew the girl was a liar and a fake – that odd moment on the stairs when she seemed to disappear in front of him, and that strange acrid smell that hung in the air. He thought, too, about how she hadn't borne a mark after that night when he had taken her, how she had said nothing to Mrs Weir and how the room was exactly as it should have been afterwards. She had clearly thought out all of those things beforehand to disturb and baffle him. It was all part of a plan. It had almost worked, too.

He wondered again whether she was consciously lying or whether she really *believed* what she had said about being Nancy's daughter. She must have known the real Grace Johnson. Probably she, too, had been at Quarrier's when Grace was there. That's where she would have heard the story: that was the only way she could have known so much. Perhaps the story had played on her mind. Perhaps she, herself, was mad or disturbed. It was quite possible she had somehow convinced herself that the story was completely true.

It didn't matter either way. She had no power over him now.

Mrs Weir was quite shaken by the events of that day. She had been exhausted and disturbed by her conversation with Clair MacIndoe. She felt sorry for the woman. And she couldn't get that image of the sleeve pinned up at the elbow out of her mind. But, equally, she didn't like what Clair MacIndoe was going to do. It made her feel sick. When Simmie asked her what Clair had wanted, she'd been vague. She didn't even like to talk to Simmie about what was in Clair MacIndoe's mind.

Renwick's return might have made her feel better if he had looked more human or if he'd behaved more normally. She'd gone up to see him when he came back but she could get no sense out of him. His words were slurred and some of what he said made no sense at all. He seemed totally unaware of this. She'd only spoken to him for a few moments but it had been quite an upsetting experience. He looked terrible. He hadn't shaved for days. His clothes were dirty. He kept smiling but it was an unnerving smile which came and went with no regard to what he was saying. He did ask about the girl. Mrs Weir told him Grace was still there and was fine. She tried to tell him about Clair MacIndoe but he wouldn't listen and she doubted whether he took any of it in.

Simmie and the girl were waiting for her news when she came back down to the kitchen. She didn't say much, just that he seemed even worse than before. She was no longer trying to hide her concern from the girl: that wouldn't have been possible now anyway.

181

Simmie drifted back to his potting shed. The girl made Mrs Weir some fresh tea. As the afternoon went on, Mrs Weir began to feel better. Things were at least clearer now. Neither she nor the girl did any work that afternoon. It didn't matter any more. Renwick wouldn't care. That was for sure. She was resigned to leaving, though she still had no idea where she and Simmie would go. The girl? Well, she would have to fend for herself.

Nancy put her coat on and picked up her bell from the table near the door, as usual. She stood at the door that led out to the garden, watching the clock. When it reached five o'clock, she opened the door, began ringing the bell and stepped out into the garden.

The girl wasn't keen to go to the dance but Mrs Weir persuaded her. Apart from anything, she didn't want the girl left in the house alone with Renwick.

They helped each other to get ready in the Weirs' cottage. At six-thirty, before they left, Mrs Weir went upstairs again to talk to Renwick. He wouldn't open the study door or even answer her questions. So, trying to put this out of her mind, she came back downstairs and set off with Simmie and the girl.

When they got to the village hall, it was already busy and noisy. Mrs Weir took a seat near the tea table, which is where she planned to spend most of the evening. Her veins were bothering her again: hardly surprising, she thought, given the tension and worry of the last few days. Simmie went off to the outside of the hall where some of the men had flasks. There would be no alcohol served in the hall, though plenty would be consumed – surreptitiously at first and then less so as the night wore on. Mrs Weir hoped the girl would have a good time, she deserved it. Grace, however, preferred to go into the kitchen and help the women there, staying well in the background.

The band – piano, accordion, two fiddles – opened with a Strathspey. The dancers went through their paces with care and elegance. It wouldn't be like that later in the evening when everyone was infected with high spirits or drink or both. Mrs Weir spoke briefly to the girl soon after the dancing started, trying to cajole her into joining in. That was the last time she saw her that evening.

The night proceeded exactly as these nights of release and celebration had proceeded for centuries. The whole village was harnessed to the same rhythm, a rhythm that would work to its climax in its own time, when the men were drunk, and some of the women too. There would, doubtless, be some love-making – sometimes even between man and wife though not necessarily so – in the darkness around the hut.

183

Mrs Weir had told Simmie they would leave at ten, before things got out of hand. Around nine, Mrs Weir felt she hadn't seen the girl for a time so she made her way into the kitchen.

The girl wasn't there.

She looked back out at the hall. The girl wasn't there either.

Mrs Weir began asking some of the women if they'd seen her. No one had seen her since soon after the band started playing.

Eventually, Mrs Weir met Innes's wife, Maisie. She'd spoken to the girl outside. She had been arriving, the girl had been going. Grace had told Innes's wife she didn't feel so well. She didn't want to spoil the evening for Mrs Weir. So she would just made her own way back. Mrs Weir was alarmed by this. She didn't know why. She was finding it difficult to move around. The ulcerated vein on her right leg was leaking. The blood would be showing through the bandage soon. But she hurried round the hall again as fast as she could, searching for Simmie, getting more and more agitated.

She found Simmie at the back of the platform where the band was playing. It was so noisy there he couldn't really hear what she was saying. He'd also had a few drinks and, when he realized she wanted to go back up the road just because the girl had gone, he wasn't in the mood to indulge her.

She was still trying to talk to him when a couple

184

of men, coming up late from Innes's Bar, rushed in and said the big house was on fire.

When people reached Renwick House, the fire had more or less gutted one side of it. The western part, which contained the kitchen and Nancy's rooms, were largely untouched. The villagers set to, with buckets of water and the hoses which Simmie had used for the gardens, and they managed to contain the fire. The flames burned with particular intensity on the eastern side of the house, where James' study and bedroom had been. At one point, there was an explosion and the flames barrelled along the corridor at the top of the house and burst through the windows, sending glass cascading down around the house. After that, the main force of the blaze seemed to go up through the roof rather than finding its way back down to the rest of the house.

As the first car, clustered with people hanging on the running boards, came up the road, they heard Nancy's bell ringing out. There was no measured rhythm now. It was ringing again and again, frantically. The flames were sheeting up the eastern side of the building, cracking like sails in the wind. Beneath them on the gravel path, dangerously close, Renwick was being held by Nancy. He was in agony, his right arm and shoulder badly burnt, the skin blackened and curling off in great strips. Nancy was trying to cradle him like a child. Some of the men, including Simmie, ran up to them, shielding their faces from the heat. Several of them found their skin burning, so intense was the heat. Instantly, they came up in great blistering sores on their faces and arms though, curiously, Nancy was unaffected by this. They dragged her and Renwick away, Renwick screaming with the pain from his arm. Nancy was hysterical and refused to be separated from her brother.

Mrs Weir stayed with them and did her best to comfort them. She asked Nancy if she knew where the girl was. Nancy just cried and shook her head.

When the police and ambulance arrived, both Renwick and Nancy were taken away. He went to hospital in Greenock. She was sent to Dykebar Mental Asylum in Paisley where she was kept, under heavy and constant sedation, for quite some time. The senior policeman in charge of the investigation was a man in his fifties called James Maxton. At first, when he answered the call out, he thought this was just a routine accident of some sort or possibly a case of arson, at the worst. Within a few moments of being on the scene, his policeman's instincts told him there was more to it than that.

The fire burned on the eastern side of the house all through the night. It continued to smoulder and smoke during the following day. Late in the afternoon, there was a sudden brief explosion from that part of the house and then, finally, the fire died away.

Grace Johnson's body was found in her bedroom. She was curled in a corner, as if trying to hide from the flames. Her body was burnt beyond recognition. In the downstairs hall, near the kitchen, all of which was relatively undamaged other than by smoke, they found the signs of a struggle – blood on the carpets and walls, and parts of the dress that she had worn to the dance. Maxton felt it was pretty clear that she had come back to leave but had been discovered by Renwick. There had been a struggle of some sort, during which presumably the fire had started. Perhaps he had been afraid she would blackmail him (Maxton had already guessed at some possible sexual relationship between the two). Perhaps he simply didn't want her to leave. Whatever the reason, there was little doubt, in Maxton's mind or anyone else's by this stage, that Renwick had killed the girl. The villagers believed that to be true but they also felt that something more had happened – something unnatural. The fire had burned with an intensity that no one could understand. There was also the uncanny way that the flames took hold only on one side of the building. But then, it's hardly surprising that an event like this should immediately take on such mythic proportions in a small rural and backward community such as Millarston at that time.

Renwick spent several months in the prison

hospital at Greenock. His arm never fully healed but the pain was kept bearable by frequent injections of a cocaine-based drug. Maxton interviewed him many times. Renwick told him everything that had happened up until that night. He refused to say anything, though, about what actually happened on the night of the fire. Maxton asked him if he had killed the girl. Renwick refused to answer.

Maxton was puzzled. In all his years of dealing with criminals – thieves, murderers, rapists – he had never dealt with anyone like Renwick. He was quite sure, on a rational basis, that Renwick had killed the girl and yet, somehow, there remained a kernel of doubt. He wasn't even sure if it was doubt. But there was undeniably something missing from the argument, something which Maxton couldn't understand. He had a watertight case against Renwick and yet there was some piece of the jigsaw missing. He tried many times and in many different ways to prise out of Renwick something about that night. There was a look in Renwick's eyes that told Maxton he was holding back, that convinced him some part of the story was being withheld. But Maxton could never break through that final barrier, no matter how hard he tried.

He went to see Nancy at Dykebar. She was still under heavy sedation and he could get nothing out of her. She just sat in the room with him, ringing the bell, over and over. She started as soon as he came into the room with her and stopped when he walked out again.

Renwick's trial took place in the High Court at Glasgow in July 1935. Renwick confirmed everything he had said about the events leading up to the fire and, again, refused to answer any questions about what happened on the night of the fire itself. There was never any uncertainty over the likely outcome. He was found guilty and sentenced to death on 23 July. Maxton watched him closely as the judge intoned the sentence. Renwick quietly closed his eyes for a moment. He looked, Maxton thought, at peace with himself for the first time since he had met him.

Renwick was to be executed on the third of September. Early that morning, he asked to speak to Maxton.

Maxton was due at the prison for the execution and was already there, breakfasting with the Governor, when the request came through. Renwick was surprisingly quiet and controlled when Maxton went to his cell. There was no desperation in his voice, no attempt to stave off what was about to happen. Renwick said he wanted someone to know the truth about that night. Maxton listened carefully to Renwick's story and, with Renwick's permission, made notes.

Renwick hadn't been sure what to do about the girl when he got back to the house. He wasn't frightened of her any more. There was no need

189

now because she *wasn't* Nancy's daughter. How could she do that to him? How could she think she would get away with that? What did she hope to gain? But he had to be careful, he knew that. He had to think this through. She could still cause him trouble. He didn't understand why she was still here. If she didn't mean him any harm, why had she stayed? No, she wanted something out of this? Money – what else could it be? Unless, of course, she was simply mad.

The more he thought about her, and the intensity he had witnessed in her, and the uncanny way in which she had built her bizarre relationship with Nancy, the more he felt this was the only likely explanation for her behaviour. She wouldn't have stayed just for money. If she believed herself to be Nancy's daughter, then she could have persuaded herself that she must come here to save Nancy, take her away. How could he get her away from here without making the situation worse? If he sent her away, and she was insane, then she would simply come back again. There was no knowing, either, what she might say about him. It would only come down to her word against his in the end but he knew no outsider would give him the benefit of the doubt, certainly no one in the village nor anyone who listened to what they said about him in the village.

He was surprised by how easily he came to the conclusion that he might have to kill her. It wasn't even a decision, not really. It was simply the natural result of following through the logic. He would try to get rid of her. He would talk to Mrs Weir. But he would have to be wary. As soon as he felt he had pushed her too far, he would have to act. He gave no thought to how he would do it. He simply knew that, in a certain set of circumstances, he would kill her.

He was tired, though. Weary in a way that he had never felt before. It was as if some of the life had gone out of him. He sank into the armchair and dozed off. Mrs Weir bustled in with coal and sticks and paper and started the fire going. She brought him some food, too, but he didn't touch that.

He heard the Weirs and the girl go out around seven o'clock. He wasn't sure how much time passed but he must have fallen asleep. Something woke him. The sound of someone on the stairs. For a moment, he was back as a child and it was his father coming to deal out his punishment for whatever crime or transgression he had committed. But he remembered where he was. The fire had gone down a little. It was quiet out there now. He had dreamed the sound of the footsteps.

He was just kneeling in front of the fire to add some coal to it when he heard the sound again.

The footsteps were coming along the hall. Again, he had a sudden image of his father stepping through the doorway, filling the frame.

The door handle turned and the door opened.

He didn't recognize her at first. She was slightly unsteady on her feet and it was a moment before she raised her face. Even then, something in her face had changed. It was the sleeve of her coat that he registered first, how it was doubled over and pinned up. Clair MacIndoe looked at him bitterly.

'Whit are ye doin here?' he said.

'Thought ye'd never see me again, eh? I bet ye're disappointed. Heartbroken nae doubt.'

'Your arm.'

'Aye, my arm. Nice, eh?' She raised her arm, tugging at the pin that held the bottom half of the sleeve. 'No dae much work wi this, eh?'

'I don't suppose so.'

He could tell that she was drunk. Her words melded into each other and none of them were as precisely articulated as she no doubt thought they were. Her head rolled slightly from side to side as if she couldn't support it in any one position for too long.

'How did ye get here?'

'A friend brought me. He's waitin ootside or he's taken aff. I don't know. Doesnae matter.'

'Whit are ye doin here?'

'Whit d'ye think?'

He shook his head.

'Ye don't know?'

He was confused. She'd never spoken to him like this before. She wouldn't have dared.

'I'll enlighten ye then, shall I?'

He knew then what she was after. She could see it in his face.

'Ye've got it. A' by yirsel. Clever boy.'

He turned away from her.

'Money. That's a' I want.'

Renwick was angry. It was all spinning out of control again. He had thought he was beginning to get somewhere, sort things out. Now, a completely different nightmare was opening up in front of him. But, no, wait a minute, this could be dealt with. If it was only a question of money, then that was possible. He had money. He could buy her off. For a moment, he had even – again, astonishingly easily – contemplated whether or not it might be better to kill her. But it wasn't necessary here. The circumstances didn't require that degree of response. He could deal with this. Money would deal with this. Money was easy.

'I want fifty, no, a hundred pounds. Or else I'll tell people whit went on here.'

His breathing was faster. He was taking short shallow breaths, none of which seemed to give him enough air.

'A'right. But I cannae pay ye now.'

'I'll wait.'

She turned and walked to the door, leaning heavily on the door handle when she reached it.

'Where are ye goin?'

'Up to my room, for a wee lie down.'

Renwick thought hard. He had to get rid of her. He had to get her away from here before anyone came back. He knew what he could do. He went into his bedroom. On the wall, there was a safe where he kept a few papers and some of his mother's jewellery. He had no idea what it was worth but it must have been far more than a hundred pounds. He grabbed everything – pearls, brooches and a thick gold band. He rushed upstairs to her.

She wouldn't pay any attention to him and flung the jewellery away. She was furious and upset about something. She had flung open the doors of the wardrobe and pulled out the drawers. They were all empty. There was nothing here. Where were her clothes? She wanted to know. How could they do this to her? He looked at the empty wardrobe and drawers and the place under the bed where the brown case had been. Clair MacIndoe grabbed him with her good arm. She was shouting at him. He was trying to get away from her. He had to get downstairs. She wouldn't let him go. Her fingers were biting into his skin.

That was when he hit her. He had to get downstairs. She fell to the floor sobbing and bleeding from the nose. He raced along the dark corridor and hurried downstairs.

The front door stood open.

Moonlight slanted into the hall, cold and white. He was sure it hadn't been open before. Had they gone? Had the girl used Clair MacIndoe to cover their leaving? Should he go after them?

Maybe it was for the better this way. Maybe,

that was it all over. He might never see or hear from the girl again. He had even begun to relax a little. All solved. So easily.

The girl and Nancy stepped into the moonlight from Nancy's room. They were both wearing coats and carrying suitcases. The girl was coaxing Nancy towards the door. She was gentle and tender with Nancy. Nancy was frightened, he could see that. She was terrified by the open door looking out onto the moonlit hills and the dark unknown world beyond.

'She's no yir daughter.'

He didn't know why he spoke. Nancy stopped. The girl's eyes flashed up at him. It was too late to turn back now.

'She's been lyin to ye, Nancy.'

'Don't listen to him,' the girl said and continued to draw Nancy towards the door.

'I don't know why she's doin this. But whatever she's told ye is a lie.'

'He jist doesn't want ye to go. He wants to go on punishin ye. Ye've suffered enough.'

'I'm telling ye the truth, Nancy. She even had me believin for a while.'

'She's my daughter.'

'Your daughter died of TB seven years ago.'

'That's no true.'

'I can get the records. They have them at Quarrier's Homes. That's where she wis for a time. That's where this woman – whoever she is – met her and heard her story. That's why she knows so much about ye and about us.'

'No. Don't listen. He's lyin. He's jist tryin to keep ye here.'

Nancy was getting agitated. She kept looking towards the open doorway. She dropped the suitcase. The girl tried to pick it up for her.

'I can tell ye a' about what happened to yir daughter, Nancy. I know where she lived. I know who looked after her. I know where she died.'

Grace tried to push Nancy's suitcase back into her hand and lead her outside. Nancy shook her head.

'Ye have tae come. Please, ye have tae come.'

The girl was becoming desperate, almost hysterical. It really mattered to her.

'No.'

'I know what he's talking about but he's wrong. I am yir daughter. I've come tae get ye and take ye away fae here. And I've come tae punish him and the people in this village that allowed this tae be done tae ye.'

'She's mad, Nancy.'

'Don't listen to him.'

'She believes what she's sayin but it's no true. Don't go wi her.'

'I have to get ye out of here. Please. Let's go.' The girl took Nancy's arm. Nancy jerked it back. The girl was crying now. Still holding out her hand to Nancy.

'I promise ye'll be a'right. I promise. Please, jist come. Please.'

Nancy was backing into her rooms. The girl wasn't paying any attention to Renwick. She was totally focused on Nancy. Urging her to come back, take her hand. It was painful to watch. Whatever the truth, she clearly believed that she was Nancy's daughter. Renwick could see that. Her heart was breaking with every step that Nancy took away from her. She followed her back into the room, tears in her eyes. Urging Nancy. Please, she said. Over and over. And that hand she held out to Nancy. And she kept it held out. Her voice stayed gentle, quiet. Then Nancy picked up the bell. It was a kind of defence, almost. Someone was there. She had to ring the bell. And she began. Again and again, she rang it in that same slow rhythm that she used out in the garden. Renwick was watching. The girl's shoulders dropped. At that moment, she gave up all hope of winning Nancy round. She knew she had lost. Only now did she turn back to look at Renwick. Her eyes were dark and burning. She seemed taller.

Renwick took a step back, suddenly if momentarily afraid of her. She started moving towards him.

'I wis coming back for you, anyway,' she said. She was crazy. No doubt about it. Beyond a hope. If he didn't stop her now, he would have no chance later on.

He started hitting her. And she was smiling at him as each blow landed. She went flying across the hall, battered against the wood below the stairs. And when she landed she was looking up at him again, her neck at a strange angle. And she was still smiling. Urging him on, he felt. He took her in both hands and brought down her head against the corner of one of the stairs. Just where they jutted out, beyond the bannisters. There was a crack. She gasped. But she was still smiling. And she didn't lift a hand to stop him. All of a sudden it was easier to lift her. He was hitting her against the wall. On the stairs, he thought. About halfway up. Her head. Against the wall. Holding her body. Again and again. And it was easier. She was light. So light. Her head was broken. Wide open. And then he saw what he was holding.

It was a baby. Wrapped in something white. And there was no stain. No blood. Nothing. He threw it down onto the carpet way below him. And then hurried into Nancy's rooms. The girl was there. Standing before him. Nancy was sitting in a chair, ringing the bell. The girl was standing by the window that looked onto the front of the house. There wasn't a mark on her face. She looked utterly beautiful. And she was holding out her hand to him.

'Now it's time for you tae come wi me.'

It was said very quietly. Her clothes were white like the baby's had been. Not clothes at all, he thought. Flowing white robes, he said. Suddenly, there were flames around her. It was as if something had opened up in the wall behind her.

A Child of Air

There was a darkness beyond the flames. Something made him catch his breath as he began to realize. The flames had a pungent, acrid smell that burned the inside of his nose and made him gag in his throat. He remembered that smell from the time at the top of the stairs only now it was far more powerful, utterly overwhelming. He could see darkness beyond the flames. The darkness seemed to go on and on. Then he could see something beyond the darkness. Other flames, far beyond those in the room. Fiercer. Deeper. He could hear screaming and crying. It was all distant and faint at first. But he felt as if he was accelerating towards the source of all the pain and misery in the world. He could feel the girl's hand on his arm. Guiding him. Gentle, though. Ever so gentle. She used no force at all. He was in the darkness now. Stepping beyond the first flames. And then he knew. She was Nancy's daughter, 'An angel returned from Heaven, come from God Above to punish me'. He offered no resistance. He was ready to go with her now. Even willing. It was truly as if the scales were lifted from his eyes. Suddenly, he felt Nancy's hands on his other arm. She was pulling him back. Pleading. Looking at the girl. For the first time, Renwick felt the flames bite into his skin. The pain shot through his body making him scream. The girl looked at Nancy one last time, with tears in her eyes, and released him. She was gone. The darkness beyond the flames was gone. And the flames were different now.

They were all around him in the room, sheeting up the curtains and the walls. Nancy was screaming and ringing the bell. His arm constituted only pain, no flesh and bones. And it was a pain that seared right through his body and soul. He lurched towards the flames, wanting the girl to take him with her. Not wanting to be left. But she had gone. Nancy somehow was beside him again. Ringing the bell. Cradling his head, as she had done many many years ago after the beatings his father had given him. But there was no comfort now. Or just the echo of it, rather. There could be no real comfort for him in this world ever again. Nancy should have let him go.

Renwick paused. It was twenty-five minutes to eight. The guards were on the other side of the cell, not listening. The Governor, the Hangman and the minister had arrived outside and were looking in, curiously.

He couldn't prove this, of course. None of it. Except of course, that they never found the girl's body.

Maxton said they had. Renwick shook his head. That wasn't the girl's body. It was Clair MacIndoe's. If that was the case, Maxton said, why hadn't he spoken up before this? Why had he allowed himself to be tried and sentenced for a murder which, according to him, he hadn't committed? Renwick stared back at Maxton, showing no expression whatsoever. Maxton looked at the clock. Twenty-three minutes left.

He asked Renwick, 'Do ye want me to apply for a stay of execution so that we can investigate this further?' Renwick shook his head. 'I don't want ye tae tell anyone what I've said or for ye tae investigate this until after I am deid. If ye dae mention it tae anyone, I will deny every word o it.'

The minister, Governor and Hangman were getting impatient, not wanting to fall behind schedule. Renwick gave a nod to indicate that they could come in. The minister read – at rather a trot, Maxton thought – from the bible while the Hangman bound Renwick's hands. Maxton remained sitting throughout this. Renwick didn't look at him again.

Maxton walked with Renwick to the gallows and watched him die there. The doctor's notes show that he was hanged at 8.02am and pronounced dead at 8.17am.

Maxton did nothing for several weeks. But Renwick's story stayed with him. He looked at the pathologist's report on the girl's body. It was fairly cursory and told him nothing very definite, except that part of the left arm was missing. He hadn't noticed that detail before but then the report had told them nothing that was very useful in the prosecution of the case. He hadn't paid much attention to it. Besides, that could just be a coincidence.

He had the house searched again. They found

nothing. Eventually, after several months of further enquiries, he succeeded in tracking down the taxi driver who confirmed that he had taken Clair MacIndoe back to the house that night. He had waited for her for a time then given up on her, knowing that she was drunk. He had seen a young woman coming up towards the house as he left.

It took Maxton another few months before he received permission for the exhumation of the body. The police pathologist, looking at the arm closely this time, was quite definite that it hadn't been severed in the fire but had been surgically removed at some point before the fire. Dental records were also checked. Clair MacIndoe had had dental work done during her stay in hospital.

There was no doubt, when the records were checked, that the body was that of Clair MacIndoe and not of the young woman, Grace Johnson, for whose murder Renwick had been executed.

Yet another search was made of the house, both those parts which had been damaged by fire and those parts which had not. They even searched the grounds and the small wood up behind the house. As before, they found nothing.

After almost two years, the trustees of the Renwick estate succeeded in having Nancy Renwick released from Dykebar. She was clearly no danger to anyone and there was no justification for keeping her locked up. The Weirs had returned to their cottage at the request of the trustees and they continued to look after what was left of the house, the garden and the land round about. One of the trustees had an interview with Nancy at Dykebar and asked her what she would like to do. He told her that there was sufficient money held in trust for her to do just about anything she pleased. She could live in Glasgow. They would find her a housekeeper. She could leave the country and start completely all over again. Nancy was quite firm. She had already established that the Weirs were living at the house again. She said that she wanted to go back to the house and live with them. She couldn't stay in the big house itself. That was now just a shell. No, she said, she would like to live with the Weirs. She didn't want to go anywhere else. The trustees were not at all happy about this but in the end had to agree. The Weirs were initially reluctant but acquiesced when the trustees pointed out that they could go on living there, indefinitely now, with a handsome allowance from the estate. The trustees also agreed to repair the roof and the main part of the big house so that Nancy could eventually move back there.

So, one day in September 1936, Nancy moved in with the Weirs and she stayed with them for about three years until the repairs were completed. They weren't quite sure what she was going to do or what she would expect of them, though they learned all of that quickly enough.

That first day, after the hospital attendants had brought her back, she stayed in her bedroom all afternoon.

At five o'clock, they were both surprised to hear the bell ringing. Nancy came out of the back door of the cottage and went into the garden. She walked round this just as she had always done before, ringing the bell as she went. She stayed outside for about half an hour. Then came back inside. That was the pattern that she stuck to from then until her death late in the fifties.

That first day, Simmie was out in the potting shed. He decided to stay there when he heard the bell. He hadn't realized this was going to start all over again. But they could put up with it, if that was what was needed. They had put up with it for long enough before. And, besides, what was the option?

After five minutes or so, Simmie noticed something moving among the trees on the hillside overlooking the garden. He thought at first it was local children. He had seen them there before, watching Nancy like some freak show in a circus. But this was just one figure.

It was, Simmie said, that of a young woman, carrying a case. She was moving through the trees in the same direction as Nancy, watching her.

It was only when Nancy went into the summer house that the figure stopped and Simmie was able to get a good look at her. It was, he said, the girl. It was Grace Johnson. Her eyes were fixed on the summer house. And the tears were rolling down her cheeks.

Simmie raced out of the shed and made his way, scrambling, breathless, up into the trees as quickly as he could. He arrived at the spot where the girl had been standing. She was gone. Simmie was uneasy. There had been something about the girl that made him apprehensive. He ran round to the cottage to make sure his wife was all right.

She was in the kitchen, sitting down. She had felt strange for a moment but she was okay now. Simmie told her what he had seen – or what he thought he had seen. And he mentioned his sense of foreboding.

Nancy had come back into the cottage now. The bell had gone silent again. Simmie and Mrs Weir searched for the girl outside. They couldn't see her. After a time, they went round to the front of the house and looked down the road that led to the village. Away down there, just before the trees began, they caught sight of a dark figure carrying a suitcase. And they were both aware of a sense of malevolence, as if there was somehow unfinished business to be taken care of, as if the village itself had to be punished for its neglect of Nancy Renwick.

Simmie wondered briefly about following her but decided against.

Up until this point in his story, my uncle had been quite quiet and restrained. Now, he became agitated and upset. It had begun to grow light outside and I thought that it was simply the realization of what the day would bring. I asked if he wouldn't like to go upstairs and have a rest. He shook his head and said that he hadn't finished. I waited. After a time, he continued. (I think this is probably better told in my uncle's own words. I can remember them with appalling clarity.)

Me and your aunt married in 1935. We lived wi my mother in Lochwinnoch at first. Then I got offered a job on a farm here. The hoose came wi the job and a hoose wis a big attraction to us – your aunt especially. She hated living wi my mother. We moved here in the summer of 1936. This wis after the fire and the trial. But we'd heard all aboot it doon in Lochwinnoch. When we moved up here, I sometimes felt like I never heard aboot ony-thing else. I mind that day that Nancy Renwick came oot o Dykebar and back tae the hoose. Everyone had been talkin aboot that. They couldnae see how she was gonnae live up there, gien that it had half fa'en doon. I saw the car that brought her go through the village and up the hill there, that day. I never thought ony mair aboot her though. I wasnae so interested in these things as other folk who'd lived through them, as it were. Far as I wis concerned, it wis just a case o gettin on wi the day as usual. I was workin in the field

up bye that used tae belong tae Cullen. It was
after five, later mebbe and already nearly
dark. I heard that bell then for the first time. I
wis amazed at how the sound of it carried
right down tae me. It wis as if she wis standin
right beside me. I never knew exactly whit it
wis then, of course. People told me afterwards, how she'd gone back to doin exactly
the same as she'd done afore, jist as she did
right until the day she died. After a while, I
went back tae my work. A couple of minutes
later, I noticed someone comin doon the road
up there. I don't know what it wis aboot her. I
had never seen this Grace Johnson for masel
afore. But there was somethin aboot seein a
young wuman carryin a case that made me
think back to the girl and what I'd heard
aboot her. I knew she was supposed to be
deid. I thought – this wis jist someone else. It
could have been onyone. So I didnae pay her
ony mair attention. I looked round again,
though, when she wis doon nearer me. Jist
natural curiosity. I could swear she wis starin
right at me. I let her go on ahead. I wis
cleanin ma spades and a scythe that I'd been
usin. As she got doon almost intae the village,
by the hall, she turned and looked right back
at me. I'd stopped workin. I began to go after
her, quicker and quicker. God knows why.
Soon I wis runnin. I kept lookin for someone
else. But no one wis around. I don't know

whether they had seen her and locked their doors or whether it was jist coincidence. She came on doon the street oot there, that case in her hand. I lost her at the turn, just after where Innes's Bar used to be. I wis goin as fast as I could now. Don't ask me why. When I cleared the corner of Innes's, she wis standing ootside this hoose, lookin back at me. Her eyes flashin, burnin right through me. I never saw or felt so much blind hatred in my life. And why me? Why me? What had I ever done tae her? She began tae put the case doon, watchin me a' the time. I tried tae run even faster. I was almost up tae her. The case touched the ground and that same instant I heard yir aunt cry out frae inside the hoose. My attention went from her tae yir aunt. I came tearin in here. It was too late. Yir aunt had had a baby girl two weeks before. Mary, we cried her. The baby was deid. Yir aunt had jist been gien her the breast when she gave a jerk sudden-like and that wis it. She had stopped breathin. She had been the first wean born in the village for a couple a years. Lots i the younger ones had been movin awa' tae Glasgow and other places and folk had been pleased when Mary was born, glad tae have new life in the place. I went back ootside. I ran up and doon that road oot there, howlin like an animal. There wis nae sign o the girl wi the case. We buried Mary three days later. Yir aunt was never able tae have another baby.

I didn't know how to take this at the time. To be honest, I still don't. I think I was almost embarrassed, believing that he was only saying these things because of his grief. I think he could see that in me. He sat for a time, in silence, looking out of the window at the hills as they became lighter and more clearly defined. Then he said he was going to go and sit with the body for a while. I asked if he'd like me to come with him. He simply shook his head and crossed over the small stone-floored hall to the front room where the body lay. He closed the door behind him. I waited a few minutes more, wondering about what I'd heard. Then I climbed up the stairs to the little room which I'd so coveted as a child and slept for several hours.

My aunt's funeral took place at eleven o'clock the next morning. I doubt if my uncle had slept at all.

There was a service in the village church. The church no longer has its own minister. It shares a minister with three other churches, all in roughly the same area. He's a young man, younger than myself it surprised me to find. He preaches in Millarston every second Sunday and is always available for funerals or christenings – not, of course, that there are very many of either in the village these days.

He knew my aunt and uncle well. He'd visited them at home and seen my aunt several times when she was in hospital in Paisley. This made me feel even more guilty for my neglect of them, especially her, over the years. If he had been able to go and see them, why hadn't I? I had loved her. Why hadn't I shown it? Sadly, I realize that I could ask myself that question of more people than just my aunt. Indeed, it seems as if the list grows longer with every year that passes.

The coffin stood on a trestle at the front of the small church. I sat beside my uncle on the first row of seats. There were only a dozen or so other people in the church, none of whom I knew. My own wife and children had stayed in London.

My wife had never liked coming up to Scotland. It had always seemed like a far more alien country to her than it should have done. Looking back, I think that had more to do with class than geography. She was resolutely middle class. *We* were resolutely middle class in London. But, when we went back home, the ethos was overwhelmingly – perhaps overpoweringly – working class. In a funny sort of way, I liked slipping back into that other world. She was never able to do that. Perhaps I never helped her to do it, as I should have done.

I had been glad to get away. I felt a deep sense of peace and relief as soon as I got into the minicab that took me to Heathrow. I stayed with my sister for the first night. She didn't go to the

funeral because she'd never been particularly
close to either my aunt or uncle. So there was no
one else from our side of the family in the church.
My uncle's brother and a son were there. The
others were from the village.

Only the men went out into the little church-
yard to bury the coffin. The women went back to
my uncle's house to get things ready. The funeral
itself was over quickly. That was the first proper
burial I had ever attended. I can still hear – with a
shudder – the particular sound the earth made as
it hit the wood of the coffin. The wind was getting
up again and driving fine particles of rain into our
faces. The minister read from the bible. We threw
in our handful of earth. Then we walked back in a
black group to my uncle's house. I turned back,
for a final look, as we walked out of the church-
yard. The two gravediggers, who had been mod-
els of propriety during the service, were now
working fast and furiously, jackets off, to get the
job finished before the rain came on properly.

At the house, there were sandwiches, tea and
whisky. I did my best to help but the women were
more than capable. The men left after an hour or
so. The women stayed to clean up. Then they, too,
went home.

I phoned my sister from the call box outside
what used to be Innes's Bar. I told her I'd stay
there until after supper and see her about ten, ten
thirty at the latest. I was drenched in the course of
the brief journey from the house to the callbox

211

and back. I changed again when I got back to the house.

We had a fairly subdued supper. Neither of us ate very much. I don't think my uncle ate anything. I tried to talk to him about what he'd said last night. I especially wanted to hear more about the child he'd lost and the circumstances in which it had been lost. He confirmed that they had had a daughter and that she had died a few weeks after her birth. But, when I asked about the girl with the case, he shook his head and said I shouldn't pay any attention to that. He had just been upset, didn't know what he'd been saying. He was both evasive and insistent. I had no choice, given this was the day on which he'd buried his wife, to let the matter rest until another time. He looked out some old photographs for me. These were mostly of my aunt and my family, taken by him. Some of them were taken in the backcourt of our tenement flat. There was myself, my sisters, my young father and mother. There were other relatives, too, some of whom I'd forgotten. Even in the photographs where there were lots of children, I tended to be standing by my aunt and her arm was resting on my shoulder or draped round my neck. He let me take some of these. He said I could have all of them but I couldn't take more than a token few. I didn't even want to take those, not then anyway.

I left at nine o'clock. I said I'd see him again soon, that it wouldn't be so long this time. He nodded and shook my hand. I drove off, down that narrow track back onto the main road, glad – I'm afraid – to get away.

My uncle died two months later. I had not been back.

To my surprise, I was the executor of their wills. I was also the main beneficiary. I now therefore own the house in Millarston. We use it sometimes for holidays. I come here to write occasionally. That's where I'm staying at the moment and it's where I'm writing these words, in the front room, on the same table where my aunt's open coffin lay.

When I was clearing through the papers, I found an envelope tucked away at the back of the rolltop cabinet which stands against the wall behind me. Inside it, there were two pieces of paper – a birth certificate and a death certificate, dated two weeks apart. They are for a girl, posthumously christened Mary – the minister's black ink has been added to the bottom of the birth certificate.

The death certificate is dated 8 September 1936. I checked with the records at Dykebar. That's exactly the same day on which Nancy Renwick was released but, of course, this in itself proves nothing.

There was, apparently, one other possible sighting of the girl on that day. Innes, the publican, had been returning to the village after a lunch with one of his wholesalers. As he came towards the turnoff for the village, there was a bend in the road. He swore that, as he came round there, he passed the figure of a young woman, carrying a case, heading up the main road to Glasgow. He saw her face and had seen her before and said that it was without doubt the girl who'd called herself Grace Johnson. He pulled the van to a halt, quite shaken by this. He wasn't sure about turning back, especially as he was alone, but his curiosity got the better of him. When he did so, he couldn't find her. He cruised up the road for a mile or more and came back down again, equally slowly. The road and the countryside all round were completely empty. There was no sign of her.